Dedication

To my husband, Chris, who continuously encourages me in this writing endeavor.

And to my first art teacher, Mr. Larry Carroll, 1944-2016.

THE MISSING BUTLER

"IT WAS THAT butler fellow that did it. Robbed me blind of ten thousand pounds" Those were nearly the last words of Abigail Rochelle who lived at No. 1 Rochelle Lane, aptly named since Miss Abigail Rochelle was the only resident on the lane.

Miss Rochelle was a spinster, a short, plump woman. She plopped a pan of brownies down on the inspector's newly polished desk. The look of satisfaction spread across her face as she told the inspector she loved to bake—an excellent hobby to have, since her portly appearance suggested she also loved to eat.

It was Nigel Brown's first case as inspector, having only been promoted the day before.

Miss Rochelle arrived at his office early. She stormed in, carrying a pan of brownies, exclaiming, "It was that butler fellow that did it."

"Pardon me, madam," the inspector apologized. "I haven't had time to move everything in yet." He removed a box from the chair and pulled it up for the woman. "Please have a seat."

Inspector Brown eased into his own chair, giving Miss Rochelle a once over. Careful observation was important in his job. He sat at his sparse desk, a blank report before him, as he glowed with anticipation in beginning his first case as inspector.

He had just taken down the details of the agitated Miss Rochelle when his ballpoint pen gave up the ghost.

"Drat! Excuse me, if you please, madam. Might I get you a spot of tea while I'm up?"

"A bit of milk to go with it, if you don't mind. Tea would go nicely with the brownies. Extra gooey I made them. I'm not one to skimp on the ingredients." She glowed with pride. The inspector picked up a brownie and took a bite.

"You certainly don't. This may be the best brownie I've ever tasted. I won't be long," said the inspector. Miss Rochelle fanned her face, which had turned bright red with the compliment.

"No sugar, though," she said as he was walking away. "I'm watching my weight." Those were the exact last words of Abigail Rochelle.

Inspector Brown sauntered over to his old desk, rummaging through the drawer and found a handful of pens. "Surely, one of these will do the trick," he muttered to himself.

Routine habit led him towards the teapot, but he suddenly remembered his new position, and made a sharp detour towards the clerk's desk. "Ralph, if you would be so kind as to bring two cups of tea to my desk, along with some milk."

Upon returning, he found Miss Abigail Rochelle slumped over in the seat, half a brownie still in her mouth. Nigel Brown's first day as Chief Inspector was not going well at all.

The one bright spot was they were close to the morgue. Poisoning was ruled out. He had eaten a brownie himself and suffered no adverse effects. That was one blessing if one could call it that. The inspector was not a religious man. Logic drove him, as did a rugged ambition towards not letting a case rest until it was marked solved, which is what got him the promotion. On the opposite side of the coin, his stubbornness in not letting a case rest for even a moment often placed him in the doghouse with Mrs. Brown.

"It was that butler fellow that did it. Robbed me blind of ten thousand pounds." It was Miss Rochelle's first and only proclamation pertaining to a crime as she entered his office, and it was the closest thing to a statement she uttered before fate played its hand. Other than her address, he knew she made some mighty fine brownies, if not deadly. She took milk with her tea, and she blushed at compliments. Not much to go on.

~~~~

The autopsy ruled that Miss Rochelle hardly had any passable arteries left. This did not surprise the inspector after contacting and conferring with the next of kin. Miss Rochelle had lived alone for many years and had no one else but herself to eat her fabulous confections.

Nevertheless, before her untimely death at the ripe age of fifty-one, Miss Rochelle had somehow been duped out of her life savings of ten thousand pounds.

Being a man with a reputation for thoroughness, Inspector Brown could not have a blemish on his record with the first case under his charge. He owed it to the dear departed woman. Of course, how dear she might be was yet to be determined. Before this was over, Inspector Brown decided to make that and every aspect of Miss Rochelle's life his business—whatever it took to bring justice. He pictured the doghouse, once again, in his immediate future.

The inspector's first order of business was the questioning of Albert Rochelle, brother to Miss Abigail Rochelle. He and his family lived in London, an hour away by train. Mr. Rochelle had been out of town on business for the entire week in question and had only returned home on the morning of the death.

Miss Rochelle's sister-in-law was much grieved to hear the news. She was already nervous and anxious, fretting over this and that. Her youngest was leaving for college she explained to the inspector. "I have been in such a tizzy, getting everything ready, you know. Well, Inspector, I should have called to check on Abigail, but I was just so busy—absorbed wholly in getting him ready. And, too, I guess I've been a tad depressed. Empty nest, you know." She looked at her husband who sat rather stoic and stiff with his spine firmly positioned against the back of the chair.

The inspector offered solace for their loss and for Mrs. Rochelle's state of mind over her son going off. "I have two boys of my own," he said, "although they won't be leaving for college for a while."

"Well, you should treasure each moment with them," she said leaning forward in her chair while turning towards her husband. "My husband is away on business quite a lot and has missed so much of their growing-up years." Her husband squirmed in his seat and cast his eyes to the floor. "And now, his sister dying. Poor Abigail. Well, just a sad situation." She grasped her handkerchief and crumpled it as if to wring out every drop of sweat coming from her hands. "It reminds us how short life is. Wouldn't you say so, Inspector?" Mr. Rochelle had settled back into his chair, easing back into his same reserved manner except for lowering his eyes a tad. The inspector made a note on his pad—*a possible sign of regret. Check out Mr. Rochelle's financial solvency.*

~~~~

"Yes, yes, you are absolutely right." The inspector tried not to betray his own guilty face to Mrs. Rochelle. The matter of not spending enough time with his own boys was another item that irritated Mrs. Brown. He vowed to himself, right after this case, he would do better. After all, he had people under him now. What was a new position for if he couldn't use it to his advantage?

The inspector made careful notes, continuing to question Mr. and Mrs. Rochelle. Neither had heard anything about a butler, she explained to the inspector, having discussed the sad and strange turn of events earlier with her husband. They both concurred that this must have been some new development.

"Inspector, it was so unlike Abigail. Abigail wasn't one to even go near strange men. She was shy around the opposite sex, never even had any gentlemen callers. I asked my husband. He had never heard of any suitors." She turned towards her husband. "None at all. Is that right, dear?"

"Inspector, it was so unlike Abigail. Abigail wasn't one to even go near strange men. She was shy around the opposite sex, never even had any gentlemen callers. I asked my husband. He had never heard of any suitors." She turned towards her husband. "None at all. Is that right, dear?"

Mr. Rochelle mumbled, as if embarrassed for his sister, "No, dear, none that I've ever known of."

"No, Inspector, she read and baked," Mrs. Rochelle continued. "Yes, that's what poor Abigail did. Oh, this whole incident is just so dreadful."

"Um," said the inspector as he continued to write.

Inspector Brown noted that Miss Rochelle's brother was on the weighty side. Must be a family trait. Mrs. Rochelle, on the other hand, was as thin as a string bean, much like his own wife.

"Poor Abigail, such a messy person," she said shaking her

head. The inspector saw that Mrs. Rochelle's place was spic and span. "My husband and I just couldn't believe how neat everything was, everything in its place, not a speck of dust, so unlike Abigail. Well, inspector, we were in shock, I tell you, in shock, but then, this whole episode has been such a terrible upset. Isn't that right, Albert?"

"Yes, dear," he responded. The husband was definitely the silent type. It was apparent that Mrs. Rochelle was the spokesperson for them both.

The inspector scribbled away between questions. "Do you think she might have hired a butler?"

Mrs. Rochelle eyed her husband and then looked back at the inspector, divulging a troubled face. "She must have. We are at a loss, Inspector Brown, just at a loss." Mrs. Rochelle had a habit of repeating herself.

"What about the bottle of wine and wine glasses?"

"Sir, my sister didn't drink," Mr. Rochelle stated resolutely, moving forward in his chair as he did so. "One drink of any form of alcohol would put her under the table. No, sir, she was a teetotaler."

"Hm, most curious," the inspector said as he continued to make notes, notes that weren't connecting any dots thus far.

"Yes, Inspector, Albert and I found that *most* curious as well."

~~~~

Albert would have been the sole heir to his sister's estate; however, Albert was a successful businessman and had no need of a meager ten thousand pounds. He had checked on Miss Rochelle's brother's finances and found him to be on an upward spiral as far as money went. He was indeed solvent. Nor would her house and possessions have been any great inheritance, not that her death was in question. Despite its new cleanliness, it was quite run down and in much need of repair. If anything its disposal would place a burden on the Rochelles.

Upon further investigation, Inspector Brown found Miss Rochelle's bank account to be devoid of funds. She had only the day before her untimely demise closed it out.

"I *do* remember Miss Rochelle." The teller placed special emphasis on the word do. "A short, round, plump woman, her head not coming too much above the counter. She came in alone," the teller related to the inspector. "Well, how could I forget her? She offered me a cupcake. I passed, making the excuse I was watching my weight. I didn't want to hurt her feelings. I could tell how proud she was of her baking. And she should be." She leaned across the counter, closer to the inspector, and said almost in a whisper, "It wouldn't be professional to be eating at my teller window. Let me tell you, though. They were indeed tempting. A true artist she was, such fanciful decorations." The teller rolled her eyes, looking over at the doorway of her boss's office. "Sticky pound notes are not something my boss would appreciate." Her voice returned to a normal pitch. "Anyway, everything was in order. I counted out the notes and said good luck with your home repair. I think it was home repair. I'm sorry. I can't be certain. So many customers, you know. Can't remember every thing they tell me."

The inspector thanked the teller for her time, placed his notes in his satchel, at the same time mulling over in his mind what he had learned up to this point. Not much, he concluded, as he walked down the street towards his office, mumbling to himself and stroking his mustache, while glaring off into the distance.

~~~~

The inspector's next course of action was to question neighbors and acquaintances. This was not an easy task as there were few of both. Miss Rochelle's house was at the end of a cul-de-sac, hidden from view by a row of evergreens and a good half-mile away from any other houses. The neighbors rarely saw her out.

The inspector, being the man of logic he was, deduced that with all that baking, Miss Rochelle must have been in need of deliveries—eggs, milk, butter, and such. Would not the butler be taking care of this for her? Someone must have seen him.

The fingerprints he had obtained had not matched up to

anyone they had on file. A description might be all that was needed to find this alleged butler.

One by one, he spoke to each delivery person. Miss Rochelle was a good customer, they all agreed. They were sorry to lose her business. She handpicked everything. She was meticulous about her baking; only the finest ingredients would do. None of them had seen a butler or a man for that matter. There had been a few smirks on the matter of a man.

J. Schlenker

The mailman told a different story. "She loved romance novels. She ordered them in bulk. The name of the publisher on the brown paper wrapping gave them away." The mailman, wanting to be as helpful as possible, added, "She liked to enter a lot of contests."

"Contests, hm, you don't say? What type of contests? Did she ever win any?"

"No, she didn't win that I know of. She sent stories and

manuscripts to publishing contests."

"And how exactly do you know that she didn't win any prizes?"

"Thin envelopes. Rejection letters are always thin," he said with an authoritative glance.

The inspector wasn't sure what bearing this had on the case, but his motto was never to leave a stone unturned. One might not know where it could lead.

The inspector confirmed that Miss Rochelle had an entire walled-bookshelf filled with romantic novels. The inspector studied his list, trying to make sense of it. She was lonely. She had some money. She was off the beaten track with her only relatives an hour away by train. She was the prime target for a con artist, a romantic con artist who liked to clean. But how did he happen upon Miss Rochelle? Was he a traveling salesman? Inspector Brown ruled that out since none of the neighbors had reported one. So, how did he know Miss Rochelle? She had belonged to no clubs. She more or less kept to herself, baking and reading. There had been no other reports of middle-aged women in the area being taken in by a con man. But then, a con man, posing as a butler, would not be so stupid as to work in the same area.

Miss Rochelle received a weekly newspaper. Paperboys are out early. If anyone had seen the elusive butler, it would have been him. The lad appeared frightened. He swore that he saw nothing strange at No. 1 Rochelle Lane. The boy's nervousness bothered the inspector, but then young chaps were often nervous around the law. He thought back to his youth, remembering his own scrapes. His parents were both shocked and pleased that he went into law enforcement. He made a note to come back later and question the boy again if need be.

Inspector Brown concluded the man in question had been there less than a week and had kept himself scarce upon seeing other people. Maybe he was truly a butler. Maybe he was as shy as Miss Rochelle. More than likely, he was practiced in the art of keeping out of sight, especially if he were playing some sort of con game. The next course of action would be to visit estates and find out if there was any word about new butlers being hired or fired.

~~~~

Another week passed. Inspector Brown was becoming more perplexed. A workload of files flooded his once immaculate desk. He shoved them all aside, in favor of stamping case number 1101, that of Miss Rochelle, closed. He stared at the notes before him and rapped his knuckles almost to the point of blood against his desktop. His wedding band echoed like a drum against the wood and left a dent. A heavy sigh escaped his mouth as he looked at the opened file in front of him and the stack of files surrounding it. His boss was hounding him. More importantly, his wife was becoming disagreeable. He had broken his promise of not bringing his work home. Sweat dripped from his brow. A bouquet was in order. Yellow roses were her favorite.

Although the flowers brought a temporary smile to Mrs. Brown's curved downward lips so prevalent over the past week, they fell short of their intended purpose. So short that he could feel them drooping towards the floor while still in his hands. The weekend was at hand. She insisted that he take her and the children on a train ride into London as he had neglected them so. For the sake of his marriage, he conceded. A break would do him good. He was getting nowhere on the case.

"Dear, I heartily agree. A train trip it is." This brightened her mood. Upon saying the words, he felt something heavy lift from him. The thought of a weekend get-a-way brightened his outlook as well. It would be good to leave the frustration of the case and the neglected workload on his desk for a while. Yes, this would do the both of them good. "Dear, I promise. I will put this case out of my mind during our trip."

"Nigel, I'm not that naïve," Mrs. Brown said as she rolled her eyes.

"Yes, dear." He could hear Mr. Rochelle in himself. Perhaps this was the way of all husbands.

On the train, Mrs. Brown chatted on about all the shops she would visit while the inspector played a game of cards with his boys. The oldest was winning. The inspector's concentration was off. As much as he tried not to, he found he was replaying over in his mind the information he had on case number 1101. He fingered his mustache and rubbed his thinning hair in disgust.

The youngest, aged ten, tugged at his coat sleeve. "Papa, can we go to the new bakery in London?"

"Yes, yes, I suppose we can," he said distracted. "What is the name of this new bakery?"

"Abigail's, I think," said his son.

"All right, if it is okay with your mum."

A light bulb went off. The inspector jumped to his feet, knocking the cards in every which direction and bumping his head on the overhead bin.

"Nigel, what on earth is wrong?" his wife asked in both pity and disgust.

Inspector Brown registered the two words—Abigail and bakery together. "Tell me Jonathan, how do you know about a new bakery in London?"

"My friend at school told me."

"Who is your friend?"

"Daniel. He was delivering newspapers. A man on his route told him about a dandy bakery that would open soon, and that he should visit it when he was in London."

The puzzle pieces were starting to fall into place. "What else can you tell me?" Inspector Brown almost screamed with a wild look in his eyes, while placing his hands on his son's shoulders.

"Nigel! Whatever are you doing?" Mrs. Brown shrieked.

"I'm sorry, son," he said removing his hands from the lad and taking a deep breath to calm himself. "This is important."

"He won't get in trouble, will he?" his son implored with widened eyes.

"Get in trouble? Son, who do you mean?" Inspector Brown gripped his son's shoulders firmly once again.

"Daniel's older brother."

"Why would Daniel's older brother get in trouble?"

"Because he asked Daniel to take his paper route. He had got sick from drinking and smoking with some other boys the day before."

This information hit the inspector like a ton of bricks. No wonder the lad was so nervous when questioned.

"No, son, he won't get into trouble," the inspector smiled to reassure his son and broke into a laugh, removing his hands.

"I know the street it is on," his son said with relief and pride in pleasing his father.

"We will go there first thing."

His wife's eyes iced over, and her mouth protruded downward once again, aware their holiday had taken a detour. The inspector recognized that look and grew uncomfortable. "Cupcakes for everyone!" He shouted which brought cheers from the boys.

~~~~

The paint was still fresh. A pale pink. An *Opening Soon* sign hung on the door. The children's mouths dropped but not Inspector Brown's. He studied the sign that hung over the window—**Abigail's Confections**. Inspector Brown banged on the door. As he did so, he apologized to his wife who stood there with folded arms. "Dear, this won't take long, really. I promise I will make it up to you."

Within a short while, an older gentleman with a paintbrush in one hand cracked the door. "We are not yet open for business."

The inspector whipped out his badge. Mrs. Brown rolled her eyes, jealous of this man who had usurped their family outing. Inspector Brown's sons, disappointed that they were no longer getting cupcakes, fidgeted behind him. The man with the paintbrush gave a puzzled look and let them all in. He put down his brush, wiped off his hands with a wet rag, and extended his damp hand toward Inspector Brown. "I'm Charles Butler. How may I be of service?"

Inspector Brown gasped. How could he have been so negligent

in missing this possibility? All the while he had been looking for a manservant or someone disguised as a manservant. He observed Mr. Butler whose face registered surprise but not a trace of guilt.

"Mr. Butler, are you acquainted with a Miss Abigail Rochelle?" He used the present tense when presenting the question to Mr. Butler. He didn't want to cause any alarm right off.

"Why, yes, I am. Do you know her? I hope you will not spoil how great this place is turning out. I want her to be surprised." Mr. Butler's face was glowing. Inspector Brown was accustomed to men who perpetrate crimes. Mr. Butler was clearly not this type of man.

"Mr. Butler," the inspector continued, "I'm afraid I'm the bearer of, well, some information."

"Is Abigail all right? I left in such haste. She was quite groggy, half asleep when I told her of my plan, our plan, I should say. She seemed so thrilled with it all." Mr. Butler's face turned a bright crimson. "We made quite merry the night before. We consumed a whole bottle of wine. We talked of making repairs to her house. She insisted on using her savings to do it. I calculated the materials needed and their cost, and Abigail withdrew the money from the bank. But, then after a good night's sleep, a most brilliant idea came to me. I sat at her bedside and told her before leaving." Blushing again, Mr. Butler looked over at Mrs. Brown in apology before continuing, "Our relationship was all above board, I assure you. When I told her of what she should do with the money, she gave me her blessing. She loved the plan, Inspector. She was still groggy, mind you, but she definitely loved it."

"Your plan?"

"Yes, this shop. I planned to call her tonight. I tried a couple of times but could never catch her at home. I was glad she took my suggestion."

"Your suggestion?"

"Yes, Inspector. I encouraged Abigail to get out more. She hardly ever left the house. I have made such progress. I took leave from work and have worked day and night on this place. Have you ever tasted her baked goods, Inspector? They are incredible."

"Yes, I have. And they are scrumptious. And, Mr. Butler, I can see you have poured your heart and soul into this place."

"I'm sorry I've rambled on. I'm just so excited. I bought the ring today."

"The ring?" The inspector's eyebrows arched.

"Well, yes, I plan to ask for Abigail's hand in marriage."

The inspector looked over at his boys. He reached into his pocket and gave them each some coins. "Why don't you go next door and buy yourselves sodas? Your mum and I will come over shortly."

"Inspector, what is this information?" Mr. Butler asked.

The inspector waited for the door to close behind them. "Mr. Butler," the inspector said with hesitation. "I'm afraid I have some bad news for you. Something has happened. Mr. Butler, there is no easy way to say this. I'm afraid Miss Rochelle has died."

Mr. Butler's smile vanished as he moved backward and turned pale. He looked like a man who had been run over by a double-decker bus.

Mrs. Brown stepped in. "Please have a seat Mr. Butler. Let me get you a glass of water." She walked over to the counter and poured him a glass. Mrs. Brown walked back over and placed the glass in his still damp hand, more so with sweat now.

"How did you and Miss Rochelle meet?" Inspector Brown asked in a most apologetic voice.

Mr. Butler sipped on the water and stared off into space before he was able to form words. "She entered a contest. You see, I work for a publisher here in London. She didn't win. But I was so enthralled by the way she put forth words on paper. I have the manuscript here. Would you like to see it?"

"No. Not now. Later?"

"Yes, of course. Well, anyway, I just had to meet her. So, I took it upon myself to go see her." Mr. Butler took the ring from his pocket, eyeing it over. "You see, Inspector, I fell in love. Do you believe in love at first sight?"

Inspector Brown looked at Mrs. Brown. "Yes, Mr. Butler, indeed I do."

"How did she die?" Mr. Butler asked in a broken voice.

The inspector explained the whole situation to Mr. Butler, leaving out the part where Miss Rochelle had thought he might have robbed her blind. Now he saw it was a total misunderstanding.

"Mr. Butler, did you know that Miss Rochelle has a brother in London?"

"Yes, she has mentioned him and his family. She told me his wife is quite the baker as well."

"Oh, I didn't know that. Mr. Butler, I will need to call on you again. Will Monday be okay?"

"Yes. That will be fine. I will have to figure out what to do. I guess I'll need to sell the establishment. I put most of my savings into it along with Abigail's. There is even an apartment above the shop. I had been getting that ready as well. I thought it just right for the two of us."

As the Browns left the shop, Mrs. Brown took hold of her husband's hand. "An incredible love story," she said, grasping his hand even firmer.

Nigel planted a kiss on his wife's cheek. "As is ours, dear, and if this has taught me anything, one shouldn't waste a moment. Life is too short."

~~~~

Early Monday morning, the inspector once again took the train into London where he visited Miss Rochelle's brother and wife relaying the odd circumstances. Together, Mr. and Mrs. Rochelle and the inspector paid a visit to Mr. Butler. Upon meeting him, they found no reason to press any charges. It was such a shame that Abigail didn't have a clue.

Mrs. Rochelle was elated with the little shop, so much so, that she and her husband agreed to buy out Mr. Butler's part. A bakery was the perfect thing to keep her busy since both her sons were now away at school.

Inspector Brown marked case 1101 solved.

The Mermaids

STROKE, STROKE. NOT the fatal or life altering mental or physical kind, but the kind where freckled, age-spotted extremities part the waters. There is a calmness in the motion, a meditation with the rhythmic movements. Parts of my body float in the saline tub of buoyancy, a weightlessness. That ends when I emerge out of the water up the ladder. The heaviness and sagging that comes with age strikes like suffocating air. But for now, I stroke. I have all the dexterity of a mermaid or imagine this to be so as I glide effortlessly in the shallow, pristine aqua water. Pristine, because my husband labors daily to keep it that way.

A pool is a lot of work. Okay, for my husband. A lot of work even for the above ground Wal-Mart variety. So much so that going away for a few days to see Jim's family causes us to fret about the condition we will find it in when we return. Still, it is one of the best investments we ever made. Some may argue that point. My family certainly did. A bunch of foolishness they said. My mom has always been afraid of water—one of the reasons I didn't learn to swim until late in life. But Jim taught me.

One day, not too long after we first met, he took me off the beaten path to the top of a hill where he used to fish as a boy. After a few beers and stripping naked with him and wading in, there was no turning back, from Jim, that is, or from learning to swim.

There was something magical about that day. When you're young and in love, you can dismiss a lot of things of a creepy nature that might be in pond water. I just remember Jim's muscular tattooed arms holding me and protecting me as my tip-toes felt the mud beneath me as I bobbed up and down, my then firm breasts sliding against his rock hard chest and stomach. I think getting the pool was a subconscious decision to recapture that magic. So I stroke and pretend away his beer belly and my sagging boobs.

I look out over the grass. I have abandoned the lawn for the pool. The grass grows wildly while I swim.

A new lawnmower might have been a wiser choice, as the one we have is on its last legs or last wheels, as it spurts and sputters across the lawn when it does start and when the belt decides to stay on. Swimming is easier. So I stroke and imagine the long green blades swaying in the breeze to be like the tall grasses near the ocean, not that I've ever seen the ocean except in the movies and in photos and other people's vacation pictures. But it is easy to imagine. Especially at night, my favorite time to swim. My mom always said I have the biggest imagination.

Yes, night is the best time. Away from the prying eyes of neighbors. A full moon tries to hide behind the clouds. I think I can see a curtain pulled back slightly, a dark figure peeping out of the window from across the road. Can the neighbors see through the tall grass over the dune? I put it out of my mind. Any thought messes up my routine. Instead, I concentrate on the minute ripples of water. The tall grasses sway in the wind; the wind and the sound of the skimmer combine, mimicking the sound of ocean waves, at least in my mind. I'm far away from the neighbors—on the vacation we can't afford.

The riding lawn mower used to be my escape into a meditative state. The hum of the engine, a trail of freshly mowed lawn followed behind me as I wove the mower around the yard like I was walking a labyrinth. But then, I wasn't walking. I was riding. No longer. The ride is not smooth—not like drifting through the ripples of the placid water. The lawnmower blades are bent. The engine no longer hums but coughs. The fairytale land of green is rough and haggard, a gnarled forest of evil beings lurking in a microsomal realm reaching to grab me with each pass. The air is hot and hard to breathe or either it rains, saturating the ground.

I always swim at night. I have to mow in broad daylight, in full view of the neighbors. They mock me as they ride past on their John Deere's, the ones with the cup holders, holding their Bud Lights, while I struggle to put the belt back around the pulleys it continuously springs loose from, grass staining my favorite yoga pants, the ones I don't do yoga in.

I make more excuses. The grass is too damp to mow. It's either too wet or too arid. Even the weather mocks me. Unpredictable. Gardens and flowers suffer. Ours waved white flags early in the season. No, the pool is much better. I can swim at night. Always at night. I am navigated around the pool by the stars.

Two frogs watch from the side. I learned my kick from them. The frogs are my teachers. When you are ready, the teacher will come. I think I've surpassed them. I know they are envious. More come. They are in awe. It's Saturday night. All croaking ceases as they stare in wide-eyed amazement. And then, one thunderous, harmonious, unanimous croak. Applause or laughter? I could just be a comedic distraction, something temporarily taking their minds off of mosquitos, the animal kingdom's answer to a comedy club. I keep stroking.

There is only the occasional bug floating on a leaf in the water. It hugs onto the gigantic raft. Another bug floats beside it. Is it pleading with the bug on the leaf? Asking to be rescued? Why doesn't the one on the leaf fly off? Is it too waterlogged? I'm reminded of Rose and Jack. There is plenty of room for the other bug on the leaf, as there was ample room for Jack on the wood that floated in the frigid water of the Atlantic. I lose my momentum as I try to save the bug not on the leaf by flipping it out of the pool. Instead, I accidentally flick it into the skimmer. Like Jack, its fate is sealed.

I return to my rhythmic baptismal meditation. My sublime movement is interrupted by a bat as it comes within a fraction of the water and a fraction of me. "Is it the full moon that draws them?" I ask my husband, who has just came out to check the skimmer. He assures me it will not bite. "That's good," I say. "I would rather be a mermaid than a vampire." Jim laughs.

It is so dark. I forgot to turn on the porch light. I can't see the edge of the pool. I don't want to hit it. I could knock a hole in it. Bats use radar to fly. I do the same to swim. The bats are my teachers.

~~~~

The weather is getting colder. The water feels like ice and stinging pelts against my bare flesh. I continue to stroke and think how handy a lingering hot flash might be, but they are long gone. My nipples are pointing towards the sky. They will be like this all day. I will never get warm. No breast-plated Viking armor will hide them. Again I think of Jack and Rose in the frigid waters of the Northern Atlantic Ocean. I can do this. The pool ladder is a few feet away. I tell myself that pain is gain. The icy water is increasing my brown fat, the good kind, and decreasing my white fat, the bad kind. I read about this in a magazine at the beauty parlor.

A pretty bird, a big bird, just flew to the tree close to the pool. It's watching me. I can't make out what kind it is. I call for my husband. "The bird may be pretty, but we don't want it," he says. It's a Gray Heron. It's after our fish. The fish pond is on the back side of the property. Now, I think it wants me. I must look like a whale in this pool. This bird wouldn't have to eat for the rest of its life. I stroke harder—must decrease the white fat.

It's exercise. Naked aquatic yoga. My arms and shoulders are sore. Each day I ask my husband if my angel wings are disappearing. Each day he lies and says yes. "But I don't want swimmer's shoulders," I say. He tells me I have no worries there.

I climb the ladder. My protruding nipples losing the buoyancy of the water point to the ground in different directions. No Viking bra necessary. A sweatshirt will suffice.

Perhaps next year a new lawnmower. We'll save up, like we did for the pool. We will have more gears and a canopy. I can ride by and wave at the neighbors with my new toned arms. No, the push kind. Have to keep the arms taut and the legs firm. The neighbors will envy my new sleek body. Or, instead, decking to go around the pool and a privacy fence. A truckload of sand for the front yard. I once heard that Brian Wilson of the Beach Boys had a load of sand delivered for his living room. No more yoga pants or gasoline to buy. I have the fall and winter to think it over. But for now, the pool.

I'm sure our neighbors are envious. Nothing says success like an above ground Wal-Mart pool in front of your trailer. My husband agrees.

~~~~

Next summer.

A group of ladies, three from the neighborhood, knock on the door of my mobile home. One hands me a cake. "We notice you have a pool," one of them says.

"Yes," I say. They look at each other and back at me. Something is on their minds. Of course something is on their minds. They brought cake.

"Won't you come in for coffee?" I ask. They make their way in, eyeing the surroundings. "Nice clock," one of them says.

"Thanks." Its sunburst points take up the whole wall above the couch. "It's retro," I add. I want them to think I purposely decorated my living room in this style. I casually mention *Wayfair.* I see the dumbfounded looks they try to hide. "It's a catalogue company, actually—online," I say. "All the latest trends." While I got the coffee table, a close-out deal from them, I omit the fact that all the rest of the furniture is hand-me-downs from both mine and Jim's parents.

I apologize for the mismatched cups as I pour them coffee and ask how they take it. One of them, Carol, says, "We totally understand. I had boys, all with their own families now. Not a cup in the double-wide that isn't chipped."

"Girls are just as bad," the one named Martha chimes in. "Pajama parties totally destroyed my couch. I have no idea what those girls were doing, and I don't want to know. I just thank God every day I made it through their teenage years."

Everyone grows quiet and takes a sip from the mismatched cups. Emily, the youngest of the group, I'm guessing to be early fifties, clears her throat. "So, we've been discussing your pool." She pauses and takes another sip of coffee. "We have been thinking about taking an aquatic yoga class."

"But our town has nothing like that. The nearest one is an hour away, too far to drive," Carol chimes in.

"So, we were wondering if we might use your pool," Martha adds. "For aquatic yoga."

"You could be our teacher. We see you out in your yard in your yoga pants," Emily says.

"Teacher?" It is now my turn for the dumfounded look.

"Yes, we could do it at night. Like you," Carol says, with a slyness in her tone. I'm reminded of the eyes that I thought were watching me from across the street.

~~~~

Later in the summer.

We have soothing music playing on a table beside the pool, as we all take our positions against the side of the pool. There are

26

six of us now, all that will comfortably fit inside the pool. We lost the desire and pretense of bathing suits early on. Only one of us, Emily, the youngest, has opted to keep wearing one.

On the nights we swim, the men have poker night. Sometimes we sense prying eyes through the slits in the privacy fence everyone chipped in to build. Emily probably knows something we don't.

We flap our age-spotted angel wings and wrinkly sagging skin into beautiful yogic movements. We've even given our group a name, *The Enlightened Mermaids*. The frogs croak in delight.

For my birthday Jim bought me a mirror, and I ditched the Starburst clock. Didn't need to see time ticking away. Instead, I hold up my arms, squinting at them in my new mirror as I walk past, imagining them to be as toned as Michele Obama's.

NINETY-NINE BOTTLES OF BEER

"SANDY BEACHES, HERE we come!" Ralph shut down his computer and relaxed back into his office chair as he watched the final seconds tick away on the clock over the doorway. Ten, nine —five, four, three, two, one.

Ralph shut everything in his office down, left an out of office message on his machine and sprinted out of the building toward the parking lot. Faith would have the packing done by now. Faith's parents had been packed since Wednesday. Betty and Barney epitomized efficiency and organization. Why then, did everything always fall apart? *No, don't go there*, he told himself. Keep an open mind, a positive thought. Maybe this year wouldn't end up as a Griswold vacation—like in the past. Who was he kidding? His optimistic race to the parking lot trickled down to a notch above a brisk pace.

When he got home, he would throw a few personal items in his bag and get the kids all settled. There would be no arguments, no giving in. They would each be allowed to choose a book to take on the trip. Rebecca would choose *Life's a Mystery*. She read that book so much, it was hardly in one piece. Noah would take one of his *Thomas the Train* books.

They would be ready to rise at the crack of dawn and get on the road, the long, never-ending road, stuck in a giant, yet cramped, van as eight adults and an eight and six year old, with luggage and beach gear, would make it so. It was really Grandma and Granddad, aka Betty and Barney, who would make it so. There would be no taking the Lord's name in vain, or foul language of any kind. Okay, he could refrain from taking the Lord's name in vain, but, darn did not qualify as a curse word.

As soon as they arrived at the condo and got settled in they would be hitting Surfer Johns. They could each pick out one beach toy. Grandma and Granddad would kick in a few extra things. That went without saying. The kids knew how to work them. Larry and Daryl would probably buy them beach toys. They were suckers when it came to the kids. Charity and Mike would help them choose.

Ralph clicked his key and settled into his car and began to back out of the lot. Just as he started to pull out, he heard a tap. It was Fred, holding up a bag, shoving it against the window. Ralph hit the button so that the window slid down. "Think about all the poor slobs carrying your workload while you're gone," Fred said, as he handed him the bag.

Ralph smiled at Fred, trying not to show pity. The poor guy probably never took a decent vacation in his life. He undoubtedly spent all of his earnings on his horticulture hobbies. His garden was his vacation in the summer months, and his greenhouse was his cabin in the snow during the winter. But then, Fred was a free agent—no wife to nag him about taking a vacation. He did have a sister, also unmarried, who lived next door. They were definitely two peas in a pod—two peas in a pod that shared gardening tasks and most things in life, even going to the movies together. Fred was also the guy in the basement office with the red stapler.

"Thank you, Fred. This is more than kind of you. I know the office is in good hands with you at the wheel while I'm gone," Ralph said. It was rather cliché, but he could think of nothing better to say.

"Actually, I'm on vacation, too, this week. Yeah, thought I'd just putter around the garden and catch up on my reading," Fred said. Ralph fumbled with placing the bag in the seat next to him just to avoid the pathetic look in Fred's eyes.

"Well, anyway, there's a little something for the trip in the bag," Fred continued. A little something was an understatement as it was a bulging over-sized shopping bag. "There are several varieties of tomatoes in there, along with English cucumbers, red bell peppers, cayenne, and chili peppers, and some cilantro. Oh, and my sister's prize winning beets." *Beets*, Ralph thought? What would they do with beets on vacation? He didn't dare ask as he would be held up in the parking lot listening to a beet lecture. At least when Fred handed him the bag, he didn't use the scientific names, as he was prone to do around the office.

Ralph was surprised Fred didn't throw a juicer in the bag. Fred was big on juicing. He once brought his juicer into the office with an array of his organic garden vegetables. He set up a juicing station on his desk, and like the lady at *Whole Foods*, he handed out little plastic cups filled with his concoctions. They were quite good. He made sure everyone tried out each of the varieties while he elaborated on the health benefits of each ingredient.

"Didn't know what your specific needs might be," Fred said as his hand slipped from the edge of the car window. A twinge of guilt shot through Ralph as he slowly continued to back the car out of the space and waved at Fred. Fred was a good guy, just a little weird. Ralph vowed to quit dodging him from here on out when he saw him in the hall. Maybe he would even bring him back some salt-water taffy from the trip. Faith always liked Fred, said she couldn't see why everyone avoided him.

Too late now, but maybe he should have invited Fred along on the trip. Fred loved to cook. Everyone adored Fred on office potluck days. His culinary genius left everyone else in the dust. He was a vegetarian, which was right up Faith's alley, and one of the reasons she liked Fred. One would never know there wasn't any meat in Fred's dishes.

Ralph could hear Betty saying, "God put animals on the earth for a reason. If God didn't want us to eat them, He wouldn't have made them." That was Betty and Barney's way of looking at things. And they could find a Bible verse for just about everything to back up their philosophies of life and religious extremism, even why Obama should be impeached. Ralph just hoped there would be no side trips on the way to the beach. They had been talking about visiting the Creationist Museum for a while now. He found himself gripping the steering wheel a little too tightly as his back tensed up.

No, Fred might be that comedy relief they all needed. He could tell a good joke, nothing too risqué for the children or off-handed that would offend Betty or Barney. One more added to the vacation count wouldn't hurt. The cast of characters couldn't get any wilder. Fred would fit right in with Larry and Daryl. They were farmers, pure and simple. They raised livestock and your basic varieties of vegetables. Unlike Fred, Larry and Daryl grew no exotic orchids with names that neither Ralph nor anyone else in the office could pronounce. No, they were just your normal everyday husky farmer type gays—gays who named their animals after female impersonators. Ralph chuckled thinking about them calling the goats. "Dolly, Cher, Liza, Barbara, come here, now."

Faith was choosy in who she picked as friends. She liked a well-rounded assortment. Larry and Daryl fit the bill, as did Fred for that matter. If Faith's parents even suspected Larry and Daryl were gay, they wouldn't be going on this trip. Nor would Charity and Mike.

Charity and Michelle, Mike for short, although it would be Michelle on this trip, were a different story. How Betty and Barney couldn't see the neon lights flashing *lesbian* across this couple's foreheads eluded Ralph. According to Betty, Charity, Faith's twin sister, and Michelle were only roommates, nothing more. Apartments were expensive in Indiana. Charity needed someone to contribute toward the rent. Guess she didn't have enough money in that massive black chained wallet she carried in her back pocket. And Michelle, or Mike, what was going on with that hair? A different fluorescent color every week. And the tattoos that girl sported. Ralph cringed at the sight of them but found he couldn't look away. What planet were Betty and Barney from? Oh, right, the tea party planet. Yeah, this trip should be really interesting.

Why Charity couldn't hook up with a doctor or lawyer and settle down was beyond Barney. Charity just rolled her eyes at his remarks.

Was the man blind? What did that Bible verse say? If your eye offends you, pluck it out? That probably wasn't what it meant. After all, Barney's eyes didn't offend him. They just didn't work when it came to certain matters. Ralph didn't presume to be any type of Biblical scholar, other than knowing the list of curse words to avoid.

Another red light. Ralph seemed to be hitting them just right. He only hoped that traffic would be easier on the trip than it was getting home right now. Any more tension associated with this vacation, he might find himself looking out the driver's window at some blonde in a red convertible.

He rolled down his window and stuck out his hand. "Up yours, buddy." Why do people insist on using their cell phones in heavy traffic?

Buzz, Buzz. He heard the sound of his own phone. "Yes, Faith, I'll be home soon. Traffic is a bitch. Yes, dear, I know not to use that word around your parents. Gotta go. Can't talk and drive."

There would definitely be no singing of *Ninety-nine Bottles of Beer on the Wall* to make the trip shorter. Nor would there be any drinking of beer in the condo—or anywhere in Betty or Barney's presence. How could he complain? It was Betty and Barney's money that had paid for the condo for a full glorious seven days. They had even rented the van, although Ralph was listed as the main driver. It was already sitting in the driveway. That meant most of the trip was already paid for. Food and gas would be the only cost. Everyone was chipping in. Still, he didn't know if he could tolerate it. What was he thinking? It all sounded so good at the time.

Fred was a beer expert, too. Made his own. What didn't Fred do? Why couldn't he find a wife? Women liked him for recipes or help with their garden, even the best places to shop. Fred was also quite the dresser. Maybe Fred was gay. Ralph had never really considered it before. Maybe he had been around Faith's parents too long.

Buzz, Buzz. Ralph looked down. He didn't pick it up. He muttered to himself, *"I can't talk now, Faith. I know I'm running late. I'm getting off the ramp."*

A few minutes later, Ralph pulled into the drive. The kids ran out to the car. "Daddy, Daddy, Grandpa and Grandma aren't going."

"What?" Ralph tried to stifle a smile.

Faith made an appearance just then. "Dad tripped while hauling luggage out to the van. Mom drove him to the emergency room. It's not a bad sprain, but he insists on not being on vacation on crutches. And Mom won't go without him. She feels like she has to stay and take care of him."

"So, we are going without them?" Ralph asked, trying out his best disappointed look.

"They insisted we go without them. The condo and van are already paid for. The kids have their hearts set on seeing the ocean for the first time."

"You're right. Everyone has already put in for vacation time. And now, we have two extra spaces."

"Yeah, we can spread out more," Faith said.

"Or, not," Ralph said as he whipped his cell phone out of his pocket.

"Who are you calling?"

"Hi, Fred. Ralph here. I was wondering...."

~~~~

Next morning

"Okay. Have we got everything loaded?" Ralph asked.

"Daddy, will Granddad's foot get better?" Rebecca asked.

"Yes, Rebecca."

"It's just one of life's mysteries about him hurting his foot, isn't it Daddy?" Rebecca said, holding the tattered book in her hands.

"You could definitely say that. Don't worry, honey. We will take them back plenty of salt water taffy."

"Ralph, I hope all the garden stuff and homemade beer I brought doesn't take up too much room," Fred said.

"No, Fred, it's perfect," insisted Ralph with a big smile.

"Can't wait to try those beet chips you were telling us about," Faith said.

Ralph grasped the wheel of the van and looked back. "Roll call. Faith, Rebecca, Noah, Charity, Mike, Larry, Darryl, Fred? Is everyone here? Okay, and we're off. Anyone for *Ninety-nine Bottles of Beer on the Wall?*"

Nine Lives

"YOU LOOK OLD," the white fuzz ball of a kitten said, keeping a cautious distance from the fat cat. The old cat, almost the same color as himself, but marked with age, sat curled up next to a bowl of milk.

"If you're looking to get some of my milk, that's no way to go about it," the fat cat replied with a sluggish raise of his eyelids.

"No, still nursing. Have no need of your milk."

"Ugh," the fat cat grunted, dropping his eyelids back down to a narrow slit.

The small kitten edged closer but toppled over on the fat cat after being distracted by a butterfly.

"Meow," came the gruff voice of the fat cat. "Why are you still here? Why don't you go somewhere else to play? Find another cat to bother."

"You don't have to be mean," the kitten said, jumping back and sliding over on its side.

"I saw your brothers and sisters earlier. Why aren't you off playing with them?"

"I didn't want to. Besides I'm the runt. They ran off and left me."

"Oh, you want to bother me then, do you?"

"No, not bother. I came to ask you questions. My name is Max."

"Well, Max, could you kindly come back after my nap?"

"When will that be?" asked Max.

"How about tomorrow? No, make that next week," the big fat cat said, hardly moving his lips, as it took up far too much energy. But Max just sat there silently, staring.

The big cat half-opened an eye and cringed. "You still here?" Max sat in silence, all wide-eyed.

"What's wrong? Cat got your tongue?" The big cat almost laughed, but his rheumatism was acting up, so he stifled the urge for any kind of movement, even his mouth.

"No, the cat doesn't have my tongue. My mama said be respectful because you're old, and she said you were wise." Max stiffened in reverence. "She said you were on the last of your lives. She said you are called Oliver, but before that was called Buddha."

"Your mom knows about me, does she?"

Max nodded with wide-eyed awe and waited for Oliver to speak, but nothing came but a low snore. Max ever so lightly touched Oliver's leg with his paw. Nothing. Max tapped harder until Oliver jumped up in a growl. "What is it, you young whippersnapper?"

"I just want to know," Max said, keeping his position, remembering what his mama said, *show no fear.*

"Know what?" Oliver snapped.

"About your lives?"

"You're a persistent chap, aren't you? Hmm, well, I've been persistent in my day. Don't get to nine lives without being persistent." Oliver repositioned himself and took a slurp of milk. "Well, I guess since you're here. Nothing else to do these days. Might as well make yourself comfortable." Oliver looked young Max up and down. "This your first life?"

"Yeah, how did you know?"

"Written all over you."

Oliver took another slurp of milk. "I go back, way back. Ever hear of the pyramids?"

Max shook his head.

"Well, they're in Egypt, a far piece from here. That was where I spent my first life. Barely weaned when an Egyptian princess took a fancy to me. In the nick of time, too. I was orphaned."

"Oh?" Max questioned in awe.

"Yes, my mama was hit by a huge obelisk. Faulty construction. Happened back then, too."

Max looked puzzled. "It's a huge pillar. Well, never mind. Not really pertinent to the story. There were human lives lost, too. Not that there wasn't law suits. Shifty lawyers back then, too. But being a cat, I had no recourse. All I cared about was that I lost my mama, along with all my brothers and sisters. But, like you, being the runt, I tagged behind. That saved my life. Maybe it was karma. I don't remember my lives before being a cat. Maybe it was just dumb, blind luck. I didn't think so at first. I just curled up into a ball and whimpered until someone picked me up. It was the princess who saved me from a life of begging."

"A real-life princess? Wow," said Max. "Was she beautiful?"

"No, not in the least."

Max looked down in disappointment.

"But not being beautiful was a good thing. At least for me. Now her sister, Neffie, as everyone called her, was drop dead gorgeous, but no, Miffen, was a little on the pudgy side. I'm sorry to say that people called her Muffin behind her back. But Muffin, I mean Miffen, had the biggest heart."

"Why was not being a beautiful princess good?" Max interjected.

"Because not everyone can be beautiful. Like I said, she was kind. She didn't have any toms all over her like beautiful women. Her attention wasn't divided on this or that, not the trivial things that interest most women, hair brushes, hair ornaments, lip rouge and the like. Time goes on, but humans change little. She lavished most of her attention on me, at least for a long time. Oh, she took in other strays from time to time, but I was her first and was always dearest to her heart, until…"

"Until?" Max perked up.

"She fell in love. Not with a prince but with a lowly worker, a stonecutter. Well, at first I thought no worries. But then, one day, she scrambled off to spy him through the reeds. He saw her. He knew how she felt. They lost all abandon."

Max sat up straighter.

Oliver paused before proceeding with caution. "We won't go into details. Too risqué for your young ears. Needless to say, I was put on the back burner for a while, so to speak. No more cuddling for me. Every day, the princess would sneak off to her lover, until her father, the Pharaoh, caught wind of the situation. Had the poor chap whipped and flogged and sent off down the Nile. Never heard from him again. Needless to say, Miffen was both miffed and sad. She drowned her sorrows in food. She must have thought I was sad too because she shared everything with me. Hardly let me leave her lap. Rubbed my fur to the point of falling out. Miffen and I both grew old and fat."

"And then what?" Max asked.

"That was it. End of story. I died, a fat old cat, curled up on Miffen's lap. I was determined not to be fat in the next life."

"Were you?" asked Max.

"No, not at all. Never got the chance. Got loads of exercise in the next life. Yep, went from a sheltered, privileged existence with a collar of rare stones, into a life as an alley cat who scampered up a ramp along with my vagabond friends aboard a pirate ship with haggard looking scamps looking to find rare stones.

"It was on a dare. Max, a word of advice, be wary of dares. Before we could get off the ship, we were out to sea, with a bunch of burly men who treated us like the rats on board. But I learned to fend for myself. Every day was one big mouse hunt. Then one day without warning, I felt the rough edge of a boot. The next thing I knew, I was gasping and fighting for breath in the Atlantic Ocean. To this day, water scares me more than most cats."

"But you came back?"

"Certainly, I came back. I'm here aren't I? The third life wasn't much better. I was on a Southern plantation. I don't know who had the worst life, me or the one who cared for me. Not that there was much caring. The house slave, Sally or Sarah, occasionally gave me tidbits of food. Never rightly knew her name because her master didn't seem to know her name—or care for that matter. As far as my name in that life, I had none. I was just known as Cat."

"What were your names in the first two lives?" Max asked.

"Well, in my second life, a few of the pirates referred to me as Boots. That was because I had white fur half way up my paws. I kind of liked that name. The princess called me Olivia."

"Olivia? That's a girl's name."

"Yes, Max, we don't always stay the same sex in lives."

Max scratched his head with his paw.

"As I was saying, Sally or Sarah, mostly fed me in the third life. But the Missus, that was what Sally called her master, kicked me around a lot and yelled at Sally to keep me out of the house. Sally was always sneaking me in, though. I died young in that life. A dog. Enough said. The master used them to hunt runaway slaves. I always wondered what happened to my family."

"You had a family?"

"Yes, a ginger-striped beauty of a wife and the cutest little kittens you ever saw. Well, I'm sure I'll see them again someday. We always run in to the ones we know. In fact, Max, you remind me a bit of my youngest tom in that life.

"I came back into the fourth life in record time. At first, I thought I was on the same plantation. After I was weaned, I looked all over but couldn't find any trace of my family. I didn't know how much time had passed. I finally gave up. It wasn't long until soldiers came and took over the plantation. One of the men took a liking to me. Said I looked like the cat his wife used to leave milk for on the porch step. He missed his wife something awful. He called me Tom and gave me bowls of milk daily and often held me on his lap, rubbing my back. Reminded me of the princess, except his hands were much rougher. Then he left with the rest of the men. I remember him putting me down, looking into my eyes, and saying, *Sorry, Tom, I can't take you with me.* I went from pampered to begging. Lived out the rest of my days that way."

The butterfly returned, but Max didn't move a muscle. "Go on, please," Max said.

"Okay, what are we up to?"

"Fifth," Max said eagerly.

"Oh right, fifth. They say cats fight a lot, but nothing like humans. I was born under the stairs of a townhouse in England. Bombs going off everywhere. My mama huddled us all together, trying to protect us. The lady who lived there left us milk when she had it. Everything was rationed. There was hardly enough for humans, let alone house pets. Can't blame her. Sirens always going off. She was always running off when that happened. Her husband was off fighting in the war. Never knew if any of them made it out alive. I just know we didn't. The bombs grew louder, and Mama held us all together as we departed that life."

"Whew," Max murmured.

"Well, the sixth. That was no bed of roses either. The war was still going on. I was in America this time. I was in a big house with a great master, a young man. There was a Scottie in the house, too. That's a dog. The dog belonged to his sister. We got along, the dog and I. We were both pampered and knew it."

"But you said the sixth life was no bed of …"

"Roses," Oliver said.

"Yeah, roses," Max repeated.

"All was great, but my master went off to war. I was so lonely, even though his mama took care of me. She was lonely, too. Then, one day, a couple of men in uniforms came to the door. My master's mama fainted. She was never the same. I was all but ignored. Everyone was sad, including me. My master's mama died not too long afterward, a broken heart. I'm pretty sure that's what took me, too."

"Oh, that is sad," said Max. "What happened to the Scottie?"

"Died before me. Car accident. My master's sister was a bit on the wild side, a flapper, I think they called her. No, no, I'm confused. The master's mama was a flapper in her day. Sometimes, your memory goes when you get older, Max. Anyway, my master's sister had the Scottie out in a car and there was a crash. Everything turned so tragic for the family. Humans have rough lives, just like cats."

"Do they have nine lives, too?" Max asked.

"I think many more than nine. But who knows for sure? Well, onto the seventh. Things got better. I was in the suburbs."

"Suburbs?" Max asked.

"Yes, like this except with spaces between the houses and yards. A yard, every cat's dream. And no dogs. At least not in my yard. There was one next door, but they kept him tied up mostly. Oh, did that dog and I argue. I would stand on top of the fence and taunt him. It was all in good fun, mind you. We were actually great friends. There was a period when we didn't speak, but we patched things up."

"Why didn't you speak?"

"Well, it's embarrassing." Oliver hesitated. "I might as well tell you. May save you from you own embarrassment someday. The little girl who owned me liked to play tea party. She sat up a table in the backyard. Had these little plates and saucers, even had real tea and milk. She even gave me some. She dressed up like a grown-up and dressed up her dolls. One day, she took it a bit too far. She put me in one of her doll costumes, a dress no less. My name was Butch in that life if that tells you anything. Oh, did the next door neighbor dog get a chuckle out of that one. He never let me live it down. Almost cost me my girlfriend. She lived down the street. We wanted to start a family, but we had both been to the vet. We just grew fat and old together. It was a good life, though, well except for the little dress-up party.

"Are you smiling, Max? Because if you are, I won't continue."

"No sir, Oliver, I'm not smiling."

"Well, okay then. What are we up to?"

"Eight," shouted Max.

"You are good at numbers, Max. That could come in handy sometime. I'm not sure what for, but I'm sure it will. Okay, so eight. Eight was good."

"Eight, that was when you were Buddha," Max said in awe.

"Well, yes. Don't know how much of a Buddha I was, but my owners seemed to think I came to them because of some divine intervention. And maybe I did.

"Once again, I was born into poverty, out in the country. My mama was a stray. Sorry to say a hawk got her. I barely escaped with my own life as a young kitten. I relied on the memory of my past lives to guide me. I ran to the nearest house and climbed up a tree. But, I ran from the frying pan into the fire, so to speak. There were two dogs at that house.

"The woman who lived there came out. She asked the dogs what they were barking at, like those animals were smart enough to tell her. Sure, I changed my mind about them later, but at first I was none too happy with those dogs."

"What happened?" asked Max, stiff with excitement and fear.

"Isn't it time for your dinner?" Oliver asked.

"No, no, I'm fine. I can miss a meal. Please, please go on."

"Well, I didn't know what to do. I just went further into the branches doing my best to hide. The woman went back inside, and I was hoping the dogs would follow."

"Did they?"

"No. These were not house dogs. But, they grew tired off and on. The woman came out and checked several times, each time asking them what was so fascinating about the tree. Of course, the dogs didn't respond. Each time I was sure to hide. I was in that tree all day. And I was starving. I had plenty of time to think. The woman looked familiar, but it was hard to see her clearly for the branches.

"Then a car drove up. A man got out and kissed the woman. He asked her what the dogs where barking at. She said the dogs had been barking at something in the tree all day. She told him she thought a bird's nest might be in there, but she couldn't find one. While she was talking, I was studying her. Miffen! I wanted to cry out. I was so elated. Oh, she looked different, blonde hair this time around, and pale, but it was her. Same eyes. Souls always have the same eyes.

"She and the man came to the tree where I was. I was no longer scared. I let myself be seen, hoping Miffen would pick me up. Instead, the man did. I looked into his eyes. Where did I know him from? Aw yes, the stonecutter. They were still in love. I was so happy for them. And here I was, back with them."

"Aww," purred Max.

"Past lives, to some extent, repeat themselves, Max. The stonecutter was still a hard worker, lean and muscular. Miffen was still a bit on the pudgy side. But, she started taking long walks after a while. The dogs went with her. The dogs turned out to have bigger barks than bites. In fact, we became good friends. Sometimes I went part of the way on the walks. But she never picked me up or petted me. I could tell she loved me, but she had changed. I think maybe petting me reminded her of the sadness in that previous life. Something subconscious. You see, humans rarely ever remember past lives. They just intuit bits and pieces. Yes, I'm sure she associated something sad with it."

Max nudged Oliver with his paw.

"What? Oh, you want to know about the name. Well, I overheard them talking about the story of how I came to be. In fact, they told their friends. Turns out, there was a cat before me —Peaches. Peaches died of old age. They wanted Peaches to catch mice, but she just couldn't do it anymore. They lived on a farm where there were lots of mice. Lots of hawks, too. I learned to avoid the hawks.

"Miffen, not her name in this particular life, had prayed to God that very same day for a new cat. As Miffen she prayed to the gods. Now she was praying to God. Religions change, too, from life to life. Anyway, the prayer was answered. There I was in the tree. One might say divine intervention. I was a Tabby. They thought long and hard on a name. At first they said Amber. A girl's name, I thought? Maybe they saw the look of disappointment on my face. The next thing I knew, they called me Buddha."

"So, you lived to old age there?" asked Max.

"No."

"What?" asked Max, aghast.

"Like I said, past lives sometimes repeat themselves. Habits die hard from life to life. You remember I said Miffen took in strays. Well, the new Miffen, mostly, the stonecutter—and by the way, he did a lot of stonework in this life as well—took in plenty of strays. It got to the point of being overcrowded. I was always wandering off. I was nearing the end of my eighth life before I wandered off for good. I turned back to my vagabond life, just like before on the pirate ship. I got in my share of fights. In the end, a fox out in the field got me.

"I had planned on going back. I know that the new Miffen and the stonecutter worried about me, but sometimes fate intervenes. I lived a good life, had a slew of girlfriends, and got to see Miffen again. Most of all, I was happy that Miffen and the stonecutter found happiness together."

"And now, you're Oliver."

"Yes, now I'm Oliver. A rescue cat."

"What are you hoping for next?" asked Max.

"Oh, I was thinking a dog. Maybe I will meet up with Miffen and the stonecutter again. We can go on long walks together."

The Wickham

DID YOU GET it?"

"Yes, well, sort of."

"What do you mean—sort of? We are on suspension as it is. If we don't pass this exam, we'll be thrown out of the library program."

"I got what counts. At least I got the gist of it."

Kalal grabbed the book from Bulan's hand. "This won't do. It's not all here."

"Some strange creature with a ribbed forehead was in hot pursuit," Bulan exclaimed as he waved his hands in the air. "He ripped it from my hand, all the while shouting, 'It is a good day to die!' What was I to do? This was all I could salvage."

"I should have beamed to the location with you," Cand said exasperated.

"I don't think that would have been a good idea," Bulan said sarcastically, while whipping his long slithery tongue out snatching up one of the insect energy nibbler bites his mother had packed for him before he left. He swallowed with one gulp and continued with his explanation. "Everyone started out friendly enough. A cordial gent with pointy ears, dressed in blue, greeted me. He made some sort of hand gesture and said, 'Live long and prosper.' I did my best to emulate it, but lacking in digits, I couldn't quite get it right. I smiled in my embarrassment, showing my best four fangs. He just kept a straight face."

"Was he angry?" Kalal asked, hoping they hadn't caused an interplanetary incident.

"I don't think so. I gleaned no emotion from him whatsoever," Bulan said, trying to reassure him. With lightning speed, his tongue grabbed another nibbler.

"Could you stop eating for one nano second?" Kalal scolded.

"Oh sorry," Bulan said, looking down at his boots, while swallowing.

"Well, as long as we didn't start any kind of incident. Burns wouldn't be none too pleased. So what happened next?" Kalal asked. "Did you…"

"That planet is strange. Are you sure we got the coordinates right?" Bulan interrupted, looking over at Cand.

"I'm sure I was close," Cand said with a puzzled look while focusing on her screen.

"Close? Close won't cut it with Burns," Bulan said.

"Well, I did the best I could with what time we had left. Whose idea was it to stop off at Risa? That was not a part of this field trip."

"That planet does have some wicked attributes," Kalal said with a toothy grin. Both Bulan and Kalal fumbled awkwardly, their tails wagging behind them, as they looked at Cand with sheepish guilt. Cand just growled.

"Well, back to the business at hand," Cand said, being the most studious and constructive one of the three. "We have at least got something. And, Bulan, you are absolutely sure this is the planet's most authoritative literature?" Cand asked.

"As sure as you beamed us down to the right coordinates."

Cand threw imaginary darts from her third eye while rolling the other two.

"There was someone named Uhura in charge of all the planet's communications. She was reading it between rolls and cuts," Bulan said, defending himself and dismissing her feminine rebuttal.

"What are rolls and cuts?" Kalal asked.

"I don't know as I didn't stick around long enough to find out. That is about the time the gruesome creature with the ridged forehead started chasing me and threatening me with death. He had some weird contraption with jagged blades in his hand."

"Well, you survived. Did you at least get the name of the planet?" Cand asked. "That will most definitely be on the oral examination."

"Hollywood," Bulan nodded with an air of authority.

"Are you sure?" Kalal asked.

"Of course I'm sure. It was in big bold letters on a hillside, where all could see."

"We don't have long. I have the ship set on autopilot. We must start studying what we have of this literature," Cand said.

"I have already read it—in the decontamination chamber," Bulan said.

Both Kalal and Cand flipped through the pages, committing them to memory. They both looked up at the same time. A lightbulb moment. Not that they used lightbulbs on their planet. Their extra eye allowed them to see in pitch blackness.

"The Wickham rules," they said in unison.

"My conjecture also," Bulan said, giving them a thumbs up.

"We will act it out in preparation for our quiz with Burns. I will be the Wickham," Kalal said.

"I suppose I must play the villain Darcy," said Bulan.

"It's only fitting since you only brought us part of a book," Cand said.

~~~~

The rehearsals went on until their ship's computer announced entry into the Romo atmosphere. Kalal took over the controls, bringing the vessel into an uneventful docking. They all stiffened in their demeanor as Cand set the beam-out coordinates for the library's archives where Burns would be awaiting their return.

Kalal held the book forward in his three digits toward the

professor. "Sir, we offer the most brilliant piece of literature from the planet Hollywood to the library's archives."

"It's in fragments. What is your explanation for this?" Professor Burns asked, appalled.

"Sir, I can explain," Bulan said, looking to the others for support.

They all looked at each other as Bulan elaborated with wild arm gestures, hoping that Professor Burns would buy their story. "I just only made it off world as the planet was erupting into war. I was chased by a most ferocious creature, which was threatening me with death. And it's no wonder. The good of the planet has been sorely persecuted. This George Wickham fellow was greatly shunned and frowned upon by the villain Darcy."

"Yes, sir. They regarded fortune as everything," Cand blurted out. "Elizabeth was after it. Yet, she found the Darcy to be utterly contemptible, although he had it. It was all a world of pride and prejudice. You can plainly see why they were on the brink of destruction."

"Yes, they started out well enough, loving the good guy, Wickham, but quickly turned against him," Kalal said, adding his part to the mix.

The three space travelers—Kalal, Bulan and Cand—stood frozen with their digits crossed behind their backs.

Professor Burns, after a deep breath shouted, "Long live the Wickham! Passing grades for all of you."

Auld Lang Syne

WE BOTH REACHED for the melon at the same time. An oddly familiar voice catches me off guard, "Are you happy?"

Not exactly what you would expect to hear in the produce section of the local grocery store.

Am I happy about the melon selection? Am I happy the melons are on sale? Am I happy that the melons are not organic, that the local grocery store doesn't sell one single organic thing? Am I happy that when I asked if these were organic, that I was made to feel like an idiot by the middle-aged produce clerk who responded in a patronizing manner, "No, dear, these are cantaloupes." No, I doubt the familiar voice is asking me any of those things. I usually shop out of town for these reasons, but mostly for just this one reason. In a small town, one runs into people, old classmates, people whose names I can't remember, especially during the holidays, and in this case—old boyfriends. Yes, the voice is definitely familiar.

"You look good," he says. He's so close I can feel his breath on me and smell his cologne. Is he still wearing Brute after all these years? Definitely still a smoker. One of the many reasons we didn't survive together.

"You do, too," I say as my eyes drift up from the melons to

meet his eyes, trying not to belie my dishonesty.

"Is he yours?" he asks, looking in the direction of Tad in the cart behind me—the child for a split second I forgot was there.

I'm thinking, *Mine, as in from out of my own birth canal? Come on, really? I'm fifty-five, which you well know since we are the same age.* Instead, I say, "This is Tad, my grandson." Tad, three and a half, snaps away with his children's digital camera, holding it up and looking through the viewer with the same precision his father, a professional photographer, does.

Joe grabs my arm, pressing a little too hard and asks again, "Are you happy?" All the while, Tad is snapping away.

I back away, and he loosens his grip. I say, "Yes." Again, I'm lying. Well, not entirely. I'm semi-happy. I'm a suburban wife and grandmother who has never had to work, who reads too many self-help books, worries about aging, and who should have gone out of town and bought an organic melon at Whole Foods.

What happened to small talk? He could have asked me about my parents, my children, and my grandchildren. And, I could have done the same. I don't even know if he has any. I didn't even get the chance to tell him I had remarried, had been for twenty years. Something inside me said he already knew.

"I really need to hurry," I say. "Tad hasn't had a nap today." Joe stares a little while, says bye, and walks away without the melon.

"Grandma, who was that?" Tad puts his camera down in the cart beside him.

"Someone Grandma used to know long long ago," I say while watching Joe walk toward the back of the store. A flood of memories come rushing in—memories of an awkward, naive past. I hurriedly reach for a different melon, even though it is greener.

~~~~

It was my first year in college. I cried for a month and barely ate when Joe broke up with me. That was after I had broken up with him at least three times. I could always get him back, but not the last time. He left me for the girl he ended up marrying, the girl who '*let him*' because she *loved* him. When I called to casually say we should get back together, which ended up with me begging him to go back with me, he made me painfully aware of that fact. I did keep track of him for a while. It was wounded pride—not love.

After a number of years, I hear he has gotten a divorce. My divorce came early on. Joe never entered my mind once during that time. Long forgotten. So much had happened in the interim —meeting and marrying Mike not long after my divorce, for one.

Maybe I decide to go to the local grocery for some unconscious reason—one of those synchronicities. I don't know. I half expect Dan Fogelberg's *Auld Lang Syne* to begin playing on the loud speakers at any moment although it is July. Instead, *Afternoon Delight* plays subtly in the background.

With eagle eyes, fearing I might run into Joe again, I wind my way up to the checkout line, careful to avoid any more encounters. Tad, seated in the buggy, picks up his camera again and begins snapping away.

"Aw, how cute," the check-out lady says as she rings up my items. Tad aimed the camera right at her. "Is that camera real?" she asks, looking alarmed, as if a picture of her wearing her blue smock with name tag might somehow land on Facebook. "Unfortunately, yes," I say. "But, don't worry, most of his pictures are a blur, and most of the people in them are headless." That seems to put her at ease, and she laughs.

I get my wallet out of my purse with focused precision, phobic over spilling out the contents, just like in the song, although Joe is nowhere in sight. Maybe he has found someone back in the meat department to hit on. I hope he gets lucky.

Tad and I wheel the groceries outside in the sweltering heat. In my mind, it is Christmas Eve and snow is falling. I can't get the song out of my head now.

Mike is waiting outside in the Prius, windows rolled up, air-conditioning going full blast. I can see he is playing some video game on his phone. I tap on the window, and he rolls it down. "That was quick," he says.

"I'll explain later," I reply.

"Hey, what do you say we go to Whole Foods after we drop Tad off at his parents' house. They are having a wine tasting." *Why did we even come here?*

Mike gets out of the car and buckles Tad into his carseat. I hope Tad doesn't say anything about the man in the grocery. Even if he does, Mike will more than likely just laugh it off. He has never been the jealous type. I'm not in the mood to talk about it now. I watch the doorway as Mike takes the cart back toward the front and hope we can make a quick get-a-way.

I remember the college days with Joe. Why was I saving myself? But then, things could have turned out a lot differently if I hadn't. I was in bed with Mike on our second date. We went hiking on our first.

Now, we go out to restaurants or to the movies and eat popcorn on date nights. Both of us have put on weight. We talked about taking a yoga class together. Talking and watching yoga videos was as far as it got. We ate chips and dip while we watched them. The most excitement we have is when we babysit Tad.

We haven't been hiking in fifteen years. *Do our lives revolve around supermarkets?* Last weekend it was the free samples at Trader Joe's. But, both Whole Foods and Trader Joe's are out of town, as are all the good restaurants and movie theaters. So, inevitably, even if we have a date night and if we are not babysitting Tad so his parents can have date night, we end up at both stores before the hour long drive back home. Our last stop is Starbucks, one for the road. Our lives have become so predictable.

"Whole Foods, Hon? The wine tasting? You look like you are a million miles away," Mike says.

"Sure," I say, rather absentmindedly. "What about a little afternoon delight before we go?" It's out of my mouth before I realize it. Mike's mouth breaks into a wide grin.

"That can certainly be arranged," he says.

"Say cheese," the high pitched voice said from the back seat. We both turn around in the car and face in Tad's direction. Mike's thinning hair is obvious as he positions his head next to mine and smiles.

~~~~

We can't believe Whole Foods is giving whole wine glasses of wine as samples. A few people are getting quite tipsy. Mike picks out six bottles to take home. We always get six. Six is how much our wine rack holds. Anything less would look strange. Plus, there is a ten percent discount if you purchase six. We watch as the people continuously refill their glasses. Then Mike whispers in my ear, "What do you say we go out to the parking lot and rock the Prius some?"

"You want more after what happened earlier?" I ask. I can feel myself blushing.

"Sure, I'm up for it," he says.

But instead, we drive home, watch Seinfeld reruns, eat popcorn sprinkled with the nutritional yeast we bought, and fall asleep.

By the next day, with all the hubbub of Fourth of July fireworks, I had forgotten about Joe. I walk out the door with the melon and potato salad I also got at Whole Foods, as it saved me from making it from scratch; we are taking them to the family picnic. Mike, putting the finishing touches of wax on the car, looks at me and smiles, his face sparkling in the bright sunlight. He has never looked so good.

He raises his head and looks up at me with a smile. "What?" he asks.

I smile. "Just that I love you," I say getting into the car. I watch his familiar gait as he puts the wax back in the garage and closes the door.

"I love you," he says, opening the driver door.

Reaching to fasten his seat belt, he glimpses the back seat. "Hey, look, Tad left his camera in the car." We pause in the driveway to look at the pictures. "Some of these are not bad. Look at this one of us he took yesterday," he says.

"It's perfect," Our faces meld into one after all of these years.

Mike scrolls back. "Who is this?"

I hold the camera and study the picture. Joe looks so old. I wonder if I look that old. I look back at Mike. I didn't do bad at all. "An old acquaintance I ran into at the grocery store, yesterday," I say.

"Who?"

"I'll tell you later. We are running a little late aren't we?"

I expect him to be a little curious, but he's not. Instead, Mike kisses me. "Didn't forget anything did we?"

"No," I say.

He starts the car and turns on the radio. The song I can't get out of my head since yesterday, Dan Fogelberg's *Auld Lang Syne*, is playing. He's singing the part about the architect.

I turn to Mike. "I don't care if you are an architect. I love you immensely. What do you say we go hiking next weekend?"

"Really? I'm for it. I will have to get the tent out of storage. Did you mean overnight?"

"Yes, overnight."

~~~~

"Grandma, this potato salad is delicious," Tad says.

"He heard 'delicious' on a cartoon this morning and has been using it constantly," my daughter says. "And it is, Mom, but I can't say the same for this cantaloupe. It's still green."

The Plans

"MONSIEUR BEAUMONT," INQUIRED Monsieur le President, "perhaps you could start from the beginning and tell us what prompted you to attempt the theft of a giraffe from Parc Zoologique de Paris?"

All ears in the courtroom were turned towards Monsieur Beaumont in the witness stand.

"Monsieur, I was not stealing Henri. I was liberating him. It was his wish," replied Philippe with a surprised expression, as if everyone should know he only had the giraffe's best interests at heart.

"Henri?" the judge asked, returning the surprised look.

"His name, Monsieur. He said his name was Henri."

"Oh, well then," the judge said with a slight roll of his eyes before proceeding. "The giraffe talks to you?" The judge did his best to keep a respectable face. However, the snickers from the court prompted him to bang his gavel.

Monsieur Beaumont was not deterred though. "Oui," Monsieur Beaumont replied, while looking around with disbelief at his mockers.

"Monsieur Beaumont, I am told that you wanted the giraffe for a pet," the judge continued.

58

"He wishes to be called, Henri, Monsieur. And, no, I don't want him for a pet. I wished to liberate him, as I already said. It was his wish."

Uproarious laughter echoed throughout the court chamber. Another quick rap of the judge's gavel hit the desk. The judge gave a stern look in the direction of the audience. "We must ask that we treat these court proceedings with respect."

The judge looked back at Monsieur Beaumont. "Okay, so the giraffe told you this?"

Philippe sputtered and spat, losing some of his nerve, and answered with a nervous stutter, "Monsieur, Monsieur, he wishes to be called Henri. The giraffe, you call him the giraffe? Very disrespectful, indeed. No, no, that won't do at all. You must call him by his proper name."

The judge winced and proceeded. "Monsieur Beaumont, it

has also come to the court's attention that you were dancing barefoot on Jim Morrison's grave."

"Oui, Monsieur le President, it was Henri who gave me the exciting news."

"Exciting news?" inquired the judge.

"Oui, I am the reincarnation of Jim Morrison. I only wished to reconnect, so to speak. I go to his grave, in essence, my grave, whenever I am sad or sometimes happy."

"So, which was it, Monsieur Beaumont?" the judge asked, fighting to hold back both exasperation and a slight smile.

"Monsieur le President?"

"Were you sad or were you happy?" The judge gave a side-glance toward the court psychologist.

"Why, happy, Monsieur le President. Henri and I had devised a plan for his liberation. We were to steal out of the zoo in the dead of the night and hide in the catacombs. I was elated to tell my former self of the plan. That is when the gendarmerie took hold of me, and, well, now I am here." Phillippe released a heavy sigh with downcast eyes. "I fear for Henri. He must truly be worried."

"I'm sure he is. I'm sure he is," replied the judge with his own heavy sigh.

"Sir, might I approach the bench?" Monsieur Beaumont's lawyer asked.

The judge motioned him forward. After the lawyer whispered something to the judge, the judge gave a terse rap of his gavel and said, "We will take a recess for lunch."

~~~~

"We would like to call Monsieur Labore to the stand, Monsieur le President," the lawyer said.

"Monsieur Labore, you were recently fired from your job at Parc Zoologique de Paris?"

"Oui," Monsieur Labore said in a meek voice.

"Would you speak up, Monsieur?"

"Oui," Monsieur Labore shouted.

"And, you were caught pretending to be animals talking to the zoo patrons?"

"Oui."

"And what did the patrons do?"

"Most laughed. Some thought they were on television. They looked for cameras."

"But not Monsieur Beaumont?"

"No, not Monsieur Beaumont."

"What did Monsieur Beaumont do?"

"At first, he acted surprised, but he believed the giraffe was actually talking to him."

"And you were standing behind some rocks, making believe you were the giraffe talking?"

"Oui."

"Can you elaborate on some of the conversations?"

"I would tell him things, like how I was tired of being imprisoned. We concocted a plan for my freedom. Philippe was to bust me, the giraffe, out."

"Did you tell him he was the reincarnation of Jim Morrison?"

"I don't remember that conversation."

"Perhaps you didn't remember it, because a lot of these conversations took place while you were drunk?"

"Oui, maybe, but I don't remember anything about Jim Morrison or reincarnation."

The lawyer turned toward the judge. "Monsieur le President, as you can see, this whole episode has been a cruel hoax on Monsieur Beaumont. By the psychologist's own report, Monsieur Beaumont may be a bit on the impressionable side, putting it mildly."

The judge, stifling a smile, said, "Agreed. The court rules that Monsieur Beaumont must undergo weekly counseling." The judge turned to face Monsieur Beaumont. "Monsieur, I would strongly recommend you stay away from the zoo and Mr. Morrison's grave. Do I make myself understood?"

"Oui, Monsieur le President."

The judge continued, "And, might you find some sort of work, nothing too taxing on the brain, to occupy your days?"

"Oui, Monsieur le President."

~~~~

"How did it go today?"

"I am to find a job."

"A job?" the voice from the toaster asked.

"Oui."

"Might I suggest an iron chef?"

"But I am afraid of knives. You know that," Philippe stuttered. "I am afraid of knives." Philippe repeated.

"Philippe, you must overcome your fear. Pinky and I will help you. Didn't we help you overcome your fear of death? You must think about how brave your former self was."

"Oui, Mr. Brain, you are right. Mr. Morrison would not be afraid." Philippe let out a heavy sigh.

"What is wrong?" came the voice from the toaster.

"I am worried about Henri."

"Not to worry. You worry too much," came the voice from the toaster. "Chew on your mint leaves and remove your shoes. You know how those two things calm you."

"Oui, you are right. I am feeling much more relaxed already."

"Oui, and you should be, and we can free Henri yet. You must bring knives, all the knives you can smuggle from the restaurant after you obtain the job. With the knives, we will rule the world. Then we can free Henri. We can free all the zoo animals."

"Oui, Mr. Brain, you always have the answers."

"Now, today is Friday, remember to pack your 'p' foods for lunch. You have a busy day. You must be strong."

"Oui, peanuts, parsley, persimmons, potatoes, parmesan, pumpkin seeds. I must remain strong to rule the world. But…"

"Yes, Phillipe?"

"Will ruling the world tax my brain?"

Jury Duty

"ALL RISE. THE Honorable Judge Gilroy presiding," the court officer bellowed with a melodious respectable lilt to his voice from many years of practice, like Ed McMahon saying, *Here's Johnny.*

My attention was directed center stage. A balding, mustached man with a vampire-like complexion, donned in a black robe, surveyed his captive audience of somber souls before he relaxed back into his cushioned chair.

"You may be seated," said the court clerk to his right. Like obedient dogs, we kept our gaze upon this authority figure as we slid with the grace of ballet dancers in perfect choreography without the aid of Prokofiev music back onto our own hard benches.

Since the judge's entrance, silence had erupted over the room like a fresh fallen snow—no errant coughs, no fidgeting in one's seat, no bodily movements, shallow breathing at best. Moments before, the one hundred plus people gabbed away, some catching up on gossip, but most lamenting their misfortune at having received a jury summons.

I had explained to the stranger next to me why it would be a hardship to come, that of having to ask my husband to switch car pool days, so I could have the car. It's not that I needed the car, as I had my own. I just preferred his. I omitted that part since it would not further my cause. Why I told her this, I don't know, as she couldn't change my dilemma any more than she could change her own. She was in the room with me along with the other miserable souls, hoping for sympathy in any form they could get it. The man on the other side of me elaborated his own story to the woman. Unlike me, the man knew the woman. The man's wife suffered from dementia, and he needed to be there to help her. My excuse seemed lame. The woman empathized and encouraged him to talk to the clerk.

There had been lots of handshakes and friendly chitchat back and forth prior to the judge's appearance. A county of less than ten thousand residents left few strangers. I was the odd duck. I scanned the room, identifying four people I knew. Having worked out of town for decades left me at a disadvantage.

The lady behind me complained that her work was such that she would lose money. She was self-employed. A man in the front never lifted his eyes from the book he was reading. He exuded calmness in a tense room. I was later to find out he was a doctor. What would his patients do without him? His brief presence there was a mere formality. The physical therapist followed suit and trailed behind the physician out the door at the judge's dismissal. The man whose wife had dementia was not so fortunate.

One of the last to enter the courtroom was possibly Methuselah's great-grandfather. He held onto his walker, as he placed each foot in front of the other. He moved in excruciatingly painful slow motion, ebbing his way to the front, as there were no seats left in the back. The shock of the man's mere presence caused people to freeze in their seats so that no one thought to get up and give him their space. Eyes registered awe at this elder's reverence for duty and shame at their own unwillingness to be there. I dreaded his walk back out of the courtroom, as surely, if there was any justice to be had in the world, he would certainly be dismissed from duty, although I realized his dismissal would be more for the convenience of the court proceedings rather than in sympathy for the man.

~~~~

This all began at the mailbox. What happened to the days when going to the mailbox was a treat? On days gone by, there were the handwritten notes, long letters, and cards. Now, there is a plethora of junk mail and bills, both dreaded and expected. The ones beyond dread are the notices for Internal Revenue audits or the jury summons.

Months earlier, I had had a good laugh over the jury duty summons my husband had received. It was peculiar that he, who had only lived in the county for a little over a decade, should receive an order to appear for duty while I, who had lived here all my life, had escaped the fate. Unlike me though, this is not something he minded. In fact, he rather relished the idea. On the days he went to court, he returned home and related the court proceedings. District court was cut-and-dry. There were no hard choices. My husband volunteered to be the head juror on most of the days they met. Opposites attract.

Karma was swift. A few weeks later, I wasn't laughing when my own jury summons appeared. It was my husband's turn to smile. He said he sympathized with me, yet he laughed a little too loud. I wasn't such a good sport.

Circuit court was a whole different ballgame. Drug dealers were the norm, but there could also be murderers. What if I sent an innocent man to prison? What if I allowed guilty people to walk the streets? What if someone I convicted got an early parole and came looking for me?

I wasn't too keen on judging anyone. Voicing an opinion on Facebook was hard enough for me, let alone in real life.

Reluctantly, I sent my papers back in while repeating the mantra, "I don't wanna do jury duty," the same way my grandson repeats the mantra, "I don't wanna take a nap." It never worked for him, and it didn't work for me. Well, actually, it did work for him in a few instances. He's younger and cuter and more conniving. My husband grinned at me and hugged me as if I were the child. I felt like one.

~~~~

My day of reckoning had come. The Brylcreem on the judge's scant hair glistened under the harsh lights. A pasty complexion betrayed too many hours spent indoors. Opening with a smile and jokes, this man took pleasure in both his job and the spotlight.

"I know many of you don't want to be here today. We'll try to make it as painless as possible." I didn't believe him. What happened to telling the truth in the courtroom?

He continued to explain the procedures and many rules. The bailiff presented handouts. Rules, such as proper dress and appropriate conduct, were cited. I couldn't help but look over at the girl with the spiked orange hair, covered in tattoos and piercings. A separate paper listed a schedule of court dates. The judge informed us that these were always changing. There was a number to call the night before to make sure whether a court session was to take place. Later, I feared my continuous hitting of redial, hoping for a cancellation, might wear this line out.

The next item of business was the roll call. Judge Gilroy expressed the importance of roll call. Roll call determined who would receive the $12.50 reimbursement, not even the cost of gas and lunch, for being there. I wanted to raise my hand, saying I would gladly pay the court $12.50 in order not to be there. But, of course, I didn't. If anyone's name was mispronounced, no one dared say so. The only sounds were the responding *heres* and one eerie *present*. Who was this guy? Well, you know the type. We all went to school with them. More than likely, this was the one guy who wanted to be present.

Most of the names went by in a blur as I waited to hear my own, but one name stood out. It was not someone I had recognized in the four people I knew. I turned my head toward the voice. Sure enough, I peeled away forty years, envisioned a head of hair where there was none, and the face beneath the age spots and wrinkles. There is no way he could have known who I was. After all, my last name was different. My own hair had undergone the change from brown to blonde. Plus, I had my own age spots and wrinkles, plus quite a few more pounds. He could have known what my last name was from my previous marriage but not this new one. It wasn't that serious anyway. I dated him during my breakup phase with the guy who would turn out to be my first husband. No, he didn't know who I was. I was sure.

Should I talk to him after this was over? I persuaded myself to do so after mulling over a scant recollection of memories in my mind—a scant amount was all there was. Yes, I would speak to Bryan. No sense in being a snob.

Judge Gilroy went on to explain the duties of the Grand Jury. He said the people to serve on this jury would be selected randomly by the clerk. The multitude directed their attention in the direction of the clerk's voice. The clerk began drawing numbers for those who would be assigned to the Grand Jury.

Under my shallow, almost non-existent breath, I prayed to get selected for this particular jury. This seemed the lesser of the two evils. My name wasn't called.

There was a short reprieve from our wax figure subsistence, as those called exited the proceedings. It was the parting of the sea, as our two groups were divided. We, the ones left behind, Bryan included, let out stale breath and heavy sighs before resuming statuesque postures.

I looked at the lawyers. Lined up behind the polished dark wooden tables, stacked with papers, they provided a barrier between us, the downcast summoned beings and the judge.

The defendant sat at the table with his lawyer. His casual attire gave off the vibe of not taking his plight in a solemn manner. Of all the court personnel, other than a uniformed officer, he was the only one without a suit, tie, or briefcase. The lawyers were a cookie cutter lot. Same dark blue suits, same Wall-Street haircuts, same polished leather Florsheims. They obviously shopped and got their haircuts out of town. Only their colognes clashed. And there was plenty of that to go around. The judge explained the case to some extent. Not keeping up with local events, I was more in the dark regarding the situation than anyone. The keyword was sodomy. Both sides bantered the term back and forth like volleyball. Incest was juxtaposed, but sodomy was the crime. Did that word mean what I think it meant?

~~~~

Lunch came none too soon. I asked one of the original four I knew if they wanted to have lunch with me. I used my cell phone to look up sodomy. Sodomy—sexual intercourse involving anal or oral copulation. Oral? Wouldn't everyone in the courtroom be guilty? Who was I to judge? We all might as well turn ourselves in and go home or reach out our arms for handcuffs. I explained this to my lunch partner. She was surprised to learn this as well. Since she was my daughter's age, I felt like I was initiating a sex education class, although being of the younger generation, I'm sure she knew more than I did on the subject. After all, I did have to look up the word. During our too short lunch break, while we caught up and talked, in the back of my mind I plotted a foolproof plan like Walter Mitty might do regarding this particular definition, one that might even lead to a mistrial.

The judge, enlivened to be back in his moment of glory, perused the crowd. I envisioned he had wolfed down lunch and took the remainder of the hour for paperwork. Maybe I should pack my lunch next time. I could slip him some pickled beets to put a little blush in those cheeks. If not beets, a sun lamp. Satisfied that no one had gone AWOL during lunch break, he re-entered his jovial zone. "Now, did any of you wake up this morning, thinking you might want to put someone behind bars?" Why did lawyers cross my mind instead of the defendant? Could others be thinking the same?

The clerk began with the second round of names. Behind my poker face, my brain was counting down and calculating my odds. I'm sure all those with any math skills at all were doing the same. By some miracle, I had escaped both selections. My breath became more pronounced, along with the few of us remaining in the audience section. The thirty-one potential jurors had moved to the juror's box. Bryan was one of them. I wouldn't be talking to him today.

I, along with those left behind, made my way out of the courtroom chamber, both relieved and spent. It was 3:30 P.M. I had put in a full $12.50 day of work. Once home, I collapsed on the couch and tried to put the next court date which was scheduled in two weeks out of my mind.

~~~~

The next court date was upon me. Once again, I worried about taking down the phone lines with my repeated calls, hoping that the next defendant had made a deal. He hadn't. Almost the same group of lawyers sat behind the austere set of tables along with the defendant. I guessed there were only so many lawyers in a small town. The defendant reeked of confidence, dressed casually in a horizontal striped shirt giving emphasis to his protruding belly, which made me think of all the empty fructose calories in prison food. I could not survive prison. One would have thought he and his lawyer were best buds as they conversed and laughed together in quiet whispers on and off again during the whole process.

Surreal was the term that came to mind as a list of seven different arrests was given. Still, the defendant showed no worry. The charge was dealing in drugs. Seven arrests implied guilt to me. Did his lawyer expect me to believe he was merely in the wrong place at the wrong time on seven different instances?

Once again, we went through the same process. Roll call was taken. The judge once again made similar announcements to the ones made during our previous jury session. The judge asked for a second time, "Did you just wake up this morning, raring to put someone behind bars?" This would become the standard opening. Only, the phrasing might change a bit. Each time, like a broken record, my mind singled out the lawyers.

This time I was not so lucky. I made my way up to the jury box. Many of the same people that had been in the box two weeks ago were once again chosen, with a few exceptions. Bryan sat somewhere behind me, being one of the first names called. Now, out of thirty-one, thirteen would be selected. The judge asked the same questions he had asked two weeks ago. Did anyone know the defendant? Had anyone had any dealings with the lawyers on the case? Was there any reason at all anyone could not serve on this jury? I listened as a couple told about their upcoming vacations. I suspected they googled Expedia on their break. Maybe I have a suspicious nature.

After that, there was the same spiel from the same people I had heard two weeks prior. One was related to one of the lawyers, but he saw no reason that would affect his judgment. The stories of how they were inseparable as children and spent many overnight camping trips together made me think of bygone days in an era of Huckleberry Finn.

We all listened as each and everyone went through his or her varying tales. As I said earlier, we lived in a small community. It left me thinking how I should have become more involved with the people in my town.

Then a man in front of me spoke up. The defendant had sold his sister drugs. "Left her in a terrible state," he said, glaring at the defendant. My Mayberry moment passed. The judge asked if this might cause him to be partial in any way. He gave a resounding, "No." I was still trying to keep my poker face.

The different councils began their questions. "Should there be different punishments for a person who sold one drug as opposed to a person who sold thousands of pills?" There were varying answers. Basically, yes or no. My answer was a little more elaborate, "Maybe this person sold one pill, and then saw the error of his ways and stopped. So, therefore, if a person only sold one pill, then, no, he shouldn't be sent to prison." I don't think they were going for elaboration. All the while l looked at the lawyer, thinking how many pills did *you* buy from him?

The female lawyer, in her navy pinstriped suit and low pumps, and scant makeup didn't break stride. "Could you send someone to prison for twenty years in hopes that he might become reformed?" she asked, not missing a beat.

"Does our prison system really reform anyone?" I answered, or I questioned, whichever way one would want to take it.

"We are the ones asking the questions," she said, her stride faltering in her low pump heels.

I wanted to say that was a rhetorical question but kept my mouth shut. On a roll, I added, "I read about prisons in which Buddhist monks led meditations. Maybe if we initiated a program like that here, reform might actually happen?" A cold chill, not a part of the air conditioning, entered the room. And, there was plenty of air conditioning—I figured to dissipate all the cologne smells. Why wasn't there a rule about too much cologne?

But back to the questions and answers. This was not me who was speaking. I couldn't even express an opinion on Facebook. What was I doing? I would plead I was the victim of a body snatcher if asked.

A recess was called. We were left once again in that meditative silence that should be used in our prison systems, as all the attorneys and the defendant disappeared behind closed doors.

Upon returning, the opposing attorneys gave handwritten notes to the clerk. At this point, the clerk pulled out the names for the final selection. In my mind, my chant began, *don't pick me, don't pick me, don't pick me.* I wasn't picked. Nor, was the man who said that the defendant sold drugs to his sister. Bryan remained in the jury box.

Again, I was spent. After my remarks, I was surprised to get my $12.50.

~~~~

Miracles of miracles. During the next scheduled jury date, I was on vacation, a pre-planned getaway before all of this jury business began. I called in from another state to let them know that. They were probably as relieved as I was.

More miracles occurred. The jury sessions kept getting canceled, one by one. We were now down to the last three. I made the dreaded call, over and over and over again. My luck had run out.

I entered the courthouse. But this time, no one checked my bag. The officer on duty merely enquired, "Jury duty?"

"Yes." I nodded.

"Go on through," he said smiling.

On my way to the elevator, seeing the size of my bag, he joked, "You don't have a bazooka in there do you?"

"Do you mean bubble gum?" Like Walter Mitty, I wished I had said that. Instead, I said, "No."

We all gathered upstairs in the crowded hallway. The double doors to the courtroom hadn't opened yet. Something was abuzz. I saw Bryan standing in the far corner. By some act of fate, the only seat left was the one next to him. I made my way over. Time to prove to both him and myself that I wasn't a snob. "You probably don't remember me, but…"

"I remember you."

Was that sarcasm? I waited. No small talk. Nothing. I whipped out the book, *Defending Jacob*, from my oversized bag and began reading.

After some delay, the double doors were opened, and we filed in. The judge informed us something was up. Basically, that's what he said, "Something is up."

Lawyers were conferring. People were coming in and out of the side rooms. The judge told us he would make an announcement soon and disappeared into the adjoining room. Within minutes, he reappeared.

Roll call was taken. The judge made his closing speech. Today's trial would not take place. There was only one more possible court date, and if he were a betting judge, which he wasn't (chuckle, chuckle), that one wouldn't take place either. We were to call in, just in case. "But, there is no need to call until after 4:30 on Monday," he said with emphasis. Was he looking at me? He thanked us for our service in case this would be our last time together.

Joy of joys! I rebounded out the court doors, leaving Bryan in the dust, not that Bryan had any desire whatsoever to follow me.

~~~~

Again, I thought I might wear my phone out hitting the redial button. I hit pay dirt with the first call. "Your jury duty is officially over. Thank you for serving." I played it for my husband just in case I had dreamt it or heard it wrong.

My husband's jury duty ended two weeks before mine. And, now, mine was finally over. I was ready to celebrate. Mexican food and margaritas were in order.

A month passed. I pulled out a hand-addressed envelope from the mailbox. It was addressed to me. My forty-fifth class reunion *summons*. Six months to lose fifty pounds and make something of my life. Would Bryan be there?

"My God, why hast thou forsaken me?"

Murder Under the Oaks: The Co-Joined Twins Caper

IT WASN'T YOUR typical murder. It was a slow demise waiting for an orgasm that never came. An oak tree played a large part, along with its accomplice, the other oak that stood beside it. On first glance, they appeared to be in the wrong place at the wrong time. But as all things, the whole turn of events would prove more complicated than that.

They stood side by side, knowing each other since they were acorns. Now two hundred years later, they hovered tall and proud. The oaks cast their shadow over their victim, mute, not confessing to or denying the charges.

The one oak in particular had the biggest role to play in the murder, but the tree doctors brought in on the case showed their connection was much deeper. They were joined at the roots, conjoined twins if you will. Upon further questioning by the detective on the case, the doctors confirmed they could have been separated at birth. One of the doctors said, "Now it's impossible. They've lived their lives in unison for so long, they think with one mind now."

The trees underwent rigorous questioning, but neither the chief culprit nor its twin counterpart talked. The heaviest gust of wind could not rattle their leaves. They puckered up their squirrel holes and crossed their limbs in defiant silence. It was a similar massive gust of wind, a tornado, a somewhat heavy-set fellow, that enticed them to this life of crime. But he's long gone, left the state.

J. Schlenker

There were one hundred years of factors contributing to the devilish deed. Any witnesses to their strategic preparation were now silent or long dead. The oaks waited for a good century. They stretched out their limbs and developed their plan with a slow, steady determination. They always stayed in the background, no one the wiser. The whole time they buddied up to their prey, shading him, giving him shelter from that bastard, wind. They had time, more than humans did for sure. Once they made their move, though, it was precise and swift.

But karma always comes knocking. "Cut them down," said the man.

"Do you want the wood?" asked the arborist.

"No. Haul it away."

The arborist scratched his head. "Lots of mighty fine wood going to waste. Couldn't you use it for your fireplace? I see you have a chimney there."

"No, we're leveling the house after these trees are gone."

~~~~

You know those movies that stick with you? They are not the funny or change the world meaningful films. They might be the ones that would never make the top one hundred—or the top one thousand for that matter. They stick in our guts because they hit close to home. There were three, all with houses as their theme.

Home is what this is about, or rather a house—a house under two massive oak trees. I kept reminding myself that a house does not make a home. Home is where the heart is, not some four-cornered constructed pile of nailed wood.

One of those movies I spoke of was *The Money Pit*. It was the first, not the first movie made, but it gave the first sign of what was to come. We should have run out the door screaming then. I can't count the number of times I've seen horror movies and called out under my breath, "Run, run. Get away now." They never do. We were the same— oblivious.

My husband and I sat there and watched, even laughed, knowing someone had stolen our life's story. The poor couple portraying us were sinking everything they had in what was to be their dream home. It ended up being their eventual doom. We laughed, only seeing a fraction of the writing on the wall. We were still in that dream home stage.

Our house was not as eloquent looking as the one in the movie. It wasn't a two-story charming Southern style clapboard plantation house with a manicured lawn nor did it have an inviting paved driveway stopping in front of the door. It was only one-story, part clapboard, part tarpaper, devoid of any distinguishing architectural elements. It sat at the bottom of a steep half-mile gravel country lane. Our first thought was how will we ever get out in the winter? To add further misery to the equation, the narrow lane, with a ditch the size of a mini-Grand Canyon beside it, didn't even go all the way to the house. It stopped short, a tenth of a mile. I thought about having to carry groceries. What if I stumble? I could see potatoes and onions rolling down the hill. Worse, I imagined a bear sizing my groceries and me up as prey on some moonless, starless night as I walked down the patchy grassed yard. On the plus side, I thought about the added benefit of exercise.

We were young. We were in love. Things always looked rosier when you were young and in love. Things looked fixable.

The biggest selling point of the house was that it sat in the middle of one hundred acres of woods, mostly oaks, the close cousins of the nefarious conjoined twin oaks. I loved nature, or so I thought.

It was faint. But I could swear I heard them laugh through their veiny, pointed leaves while we were moving in our hand-me-down furniture. My husband said it was my imagination.

The second biggest selling point was that the house was free. Yes, it was an inheritance. There was someone who stood in line before us, another couple. You may wonder what happened to them. It wasn't gruesome or anything.

They gave it a try. Not a good fit for the house. Maybe we should have sensed something was up then.

Before them, there were generations of couples starting out here. It was a starter home. It had been a starter home since my grandfather and grandmother first built the house back in 1912. The lilies she planted still grew beside the house. Well, when we left, they were still there. My grandparents separated. Was that a sign? Couples back then rarely divorced. Was it the house? They lived in separate houses when I was a child, less than a half-mile apart, closer to town.

My own parents never lived in the house, but everyone else in the family did at one time. Looking back on it, there was an unusually high divorce rate in my family.

Back to the couple before us. They lasted one night. They had the foresight to move. They now lived in one of those brick mansions. Maybe I overstate their residential situation, but almost anything is a palace in comparison. A wagon train of mice scurrying across the floor was enough to send them packing with their bags. We went in loaded down with D-Con and a clowder of cats. We dressed them in camouflage, armed them with miniature Tommy guns and told them to patrol the perimeter. I exaggerate but not too much. I hate mice.

My caveman husband pounded on his chest saying he would defend me from them until the bitter end. It was an easy proclamation considering he was away at work in another town most of the day.

It wasn't long before I found our little feline army had flunked basic training. Maybe one reason was that the cats were outside, and the mice were inside. I tried to give them the benefit of the doubt. It didn't take Sherlock Holmes to deduce our cats were just stupid. They, the mice that is, mocked me and laughed in my face. In all probability, the cats were laughing too, especially since I was feeding them primo cat food twice a day. For all I knew, they were conspiring with the mice. Maybe I was the one who was stupid.

I had cleared the cupboard numerous times from their rampages. My anger was turning into vengeance. With paint bucket and brush in hand, trying to make the place presentable, I turned up the music full volume to annoy them. *Maybe* they liked soft rock. I could have put on heavy metal, but that would have annoyed me. With each brush stroke, I plotted their destruction. It was me against them.

Needless to say, I was the Tupperware lady's favorite person. When the plastic containers were full and spaces to store them were taken, as we still needed closets and cabinets, something old houses don't come well equipped with, I resorted to putting the overflow in the oven. We didn't have a microwave. I thought it a safe haven for my spoils.

On one of those days when my husband was at work, I hid away a bag of Oreo cookies in the oven. How could those little monsters get into something that was airtight? Right? Wrong.

The next day, I had my pot of tea boiling and favorite teacup at my side, taking a break from the painting. My mouth watered for some of that dark chocolate cream-filled goodness to go with it. I opened the oven door to find half of the bag of cookies gone or in crumbles. To my horror, the culprit was still there. It was sluggish from the added weight, lying drunk and outstretched on the cellophane bag. He or she barely acknowledged my presence. One would think my blood curdling scream might have alerted the neighbors a half mile away to foul play, and a call to the police. But, like everyone else in the small farming neighborhood, they were at work. I shut the oven door with a bang.

I paced the floor, too anxiety-ridden to think of a plan of action. They couldn't win. Of this, I was sure. I called my husband, fifty miles away. He could hardly come home to take care of the situation. He coached me through it over the phone.

"You see the fireplace shovel?" he asked.

"Yes, I see it."

"I want you to get it and open the oven door."

"Okay."

"Do you have the door open?"

"Yes."

"What's the mouse doing?"

"He's looking at me with his bloodshot green monster eyes."

He laughed. I envisioned he had me on speakerphone with the entire office listening in on the conversation. There were some days I felt like Lucy, and that my husband was Ricky. It didn't help being blonde.

"This is not funny," I retort. "I'm on the verge of tears or a nervous breakdown. I'm not sure which."

"Okay, I'm sorry. It's going to be okay. Just put the shovel in and take the mouse and bag of cookies and dump them outside. I'll take care of it when I get home. I'll even clean the oven. Did you open the outside door?"

"No, you didn't tell me that part."

I heard a snicker. "Okay, then open the door."

"Okay, I opened it."

"So, what is happening now?"

"I'm standing at the door. The dog is looking at me weirdly." I needed a distraction to take my mind off of the matter at hand.

"Forget the dog. Let's deal with the mouse."

"Okay."

"Just do it fast."

I put the phone on speaker. After several false starts, I cry out to my husband, "I can't. I can't. He is still alive. What if he jumps off the shovel and attacks me?"

"Okay, okay. I'll do my best to leave early. In the meantime it's a nice day. Take a walk outside or something."

"Okay, I love you." At that point, I was grasping for intimacy or makeup sex even though a snicker didn't constitute a fight.

"I love you, too. Just stay calm until I get home."

I didn't take his advice. I closed the oven door but couldn't take my eyes off it. *What if he escapes? How did he get in there? Is there a back entrance small enough for a mouse? Not a sound.* He was bound to awaken from his drunken stupor sooner or later. I couldn't stand guard all day. Eventually, the urge to go to the bathroom would arise. I turned the oven on broil. It had to be quick. I wasn't without mercy.

Two hours later, my husband arrived home. "What is that smell?"

"We need to go out for dinner and oven shopping," I said with a straight face. There would be no negotiation.

~~~~

That happened many years ago. The new oven led to the next project, a new kitchen with an abundance of cabinet space. We upped our cat population after administering IQ tests. We lived in one room at a time, fixing an old house that should have been demolished and restarted from the ground up. That was the advice we got when we inherited it. But, no, we couldn't afford a mortgage. Where would we live in the meantime? Not with our parents, and we couldn't afford rent and a house loan at the same time.

The plan was to live in it and fix it up as we went. We bubbled with joy at the challenge before us. We weren't like other couples. No, we were a bit off.

Before the kitchen renovation, in our exuberance to begin the remodeling, we purchased a four hundred dollar burnt umber cast iron tub. That was back when four hundred dollars was a big chunk of money for a bathtub and back when that color was all the rage. The tub got lots of use. Seeing disgusting mouse droppings off and on over the years, inspired long scented bubble baths.

Our families mocked us along with the mice. I feared even our faithful loving dogs were crossing over to their side. My father looked perplexed. "Why would you put a four hundred dollar bathtub in an eight hundred dollar house?"

To make the house worth twelve-hundred, I wanted to say but didn't.

The only thing that proved to be indestructible in that house was that tub. In the end, it was in one piece. The avocado washer and dryer lasted for two decades. I thought they would never bite the dust. There were days when I felt like I was living in a seventies' time capsule.

Our plan was the same as the oaks. We would take care of one item at a time. We were in it for the duration. The movie was becoming more real.

~~~~

Soon it was time to halt the projects and concentrate on one. I held up the Popsicle stick of plastic with the window showing two pink lines for my husband to see. We faced a new challenge— fitting a nursery into the cramped dwelling. When our second, a boy, came along, we added a room. Our third was also a boy. We carted in bunk beds. Our daughter retained the nursery.

Like most kids, they liked sweets. I was blending wheat grass and kale in my Vita-Mix before it was in vogue. They were snarling their noses in disgust. We couldn't sequester them from the Oreo commercials on television. They didn't understand why they were being denied. Their friends ate them. We offered them no explanation. Deep down, we feared they might run away from home. On Halloween, we threw some caramel apples into the mix with the usual granola bars. We suspected their grandparents were going against our wishes and sneaking them all sorts of sugar monstrosities. We offered the grandparents no explanation for our odd behavior. Strange behavior was something they came to expect from us.

One day, my youngest had company over. "Why won't your mom let you eat Oreos?" I overheard one boy ask.

He did what any quick thinking pre-teen would do and said, "I'm allergic."

The other kid shrugged. "Oh, that explains why you can't even have them in the house. I'm allergic to spinach myself. My mom isn't so nice. She still serves it at dinner time."

~~~~

The second movie that should have been a sign was *Burnt Offerings*. It starred Betty Davis. A family moves into an old house that needs a life force to rejuvenate itself. The house chose one family member to drain the energy from and held that person prisoner. The rest of the family members were killed off. Maybe we staved off any killing by offering up the mouse. Still, the house sucked the energy out of us.

We struggled along for decades. We raised a family with only wood burning stoves as heat and no air conditioning. We ignored their pleas to live in suburbia where there were neighbor kids with which to play. We told them to count their blessings. They had beautiful wooded hills and creeks as their playground. When they whined, we threatened to homeschool them. Why couldn't they accept things as they were? Wednesday and Pugsley did.

They grew up and moved hundreds of miles away to big cities, into the cookie-cutter houses, the kind we always professed to detest. In secret, we were rethinking our stance. There, our grandchildren rode their bicycles and played basketball on asphalt streets with the other neighbor children. We begged our kids to bring the grandkids for a visit. They declined most of the time. When they came, they planned their visits after heavy downpours when they knew there would be enough water in the cisterns for everyone to have long showers.

We never took time off. We worked on weekends. We were on a first name basis with Home Depot and Lowe's. At this point, I would have to throw the television program *Green Acres* into the mix. You would have to compare our work standards to those of Ralph and Alf Monroe. It was a slow process that never ended.

One of the most annoying questions that people constantly asked was, "Is the house finished yet?"

We never came up with an answer to that. One reason the work resembled that of the Monroe's is that we often let the kids help with certain projects. Did I say let? They called it forceful coercion. They were so eager as toddlers to help. They got out their little plastic tool sets, with their fake tool belts fastened around their tiny waists, begging to be let in on the fun. They saw things differently as teenagers. They begged for reprieves from the work. Couldn't they go to movies with their friends like normal teenagers? We caved into their demands more than they liked to admit.

The first project they did with us, they loved. The whole venture was a project of love. On that piece of ground in front of the house that defied lawn mowers, we dug a small hole and made a fishpond. It became our spring project. Each year the hole got bigger. We added rocks and made the waterfall bigger. We watched the Koi grow along with the children. We planted small shrubs around it, and they grew along with the children, as well. Each year we added something different. We even built a glider swing that overlooked it. Of all our undertakings, it was our masterpiece.

We saw the work as character building. Wouldn't they love a beautiful new deck? They could invite their friends over for pizza parties. "I don't think so," they all said. "Our friends don't want to come here. You'll have them help build the pizza oven."

The deck did get finished, and there was an indentation in it so as not to disturb the oaks. You would think they would have appreciated our respect for them. Instead, they bombed us with acorns. Our kids used the deck, rather profusely. They rode their bicycles across it. They put up a tent on it, spending many nights there, telling ghost stories. I knew the oaks eavesdropped. I theorized the ghost stories spurred them on toward their propensity for evil.

~~~~

The third movie was *Amityville Horror*. With this revelation, you might think the house was cursed or haunted. We never saw ghosts, but there were warnings that it might be cursed. Weeks before the mighty oaks made their move, there were flies, not hundreds but enough. I tried everything, incense, scented candles, various oil fragrances, which were supposed to repel them. Nothing worked. I thanked God we had no basement, only a tight crawlspace that neither man nor beast could slither through in certain sections.

~~~~

When all was said and done, it was the tornado like fellow who made an appearance. There was some kind of brawl. We listened to them arguing, but in the end the oaks conspired with the tornado like fellow to destroy the house.

The oaks beat their limbs against the house. We had never heard such a ruckus. A good portion of the roof came tumbling down around us. Our lives were spared. We sat up in bed, cold, wet, and covered in sheetrock dust and cedar shake shingles. The deck was gone. It would have to be rebuilt.

Instead of calling our children or driving to the nearest motel, we lingered in our pajamas and discussed a skylight where the hole in the roof was. When our kids found out, they trekked to our house, descending upon us like they were the ones who were in charge. It was the first time we've had them all gathered at once at their childhood home since marrying and having their own families. They held an intervention beneath the same culprits that had caused all this chaos.

Our children threatened to commit us. We reminded them we could have homeschooled them but didn't. They relented. Then they departed back to Motel 6.

We closed off the side of the house that took the hit, covered the roof with plastic, and moved into the other bedroom. On the next day, the kids and grandchildren returned. They announced they had an early anniversary present for us. They pooled their resources. They led us outside where a tenth of a mile up from the house in the driveway a Sportscoach Pathfinder motor home was parked.

"Mom, Dad, it has all the amenities of home," our daughter said.

"Well, actually better," our youngest son said.

"With the sale of the land," our middle son said. His father gave him a stern look, but he went on, "and house, you should have a tidy sum."

"Don't forget most of the furnishings and tools. The tools alone should bring in a lot," our daughter chimed in.

A new tool had been the standard present for birthdays, Christmas, anniversaries, and yes, even Valentine's Day.

"What we are trying to say," our middle son continued, "is that you should have enough to live off of for the rest of your days."

"It will be the vacation you never took; *we* never took," our youngest said.

We stood looking at them, like the oaks. Only, we didn't have a plan like the oaks. We were numb. They kept waiting for a response. While they stood waiting, we told them we needed to talk and walked back down to the house. We went through the rooms, one by one, all nine of them if you counted hallways. We looked up at what was once the ceiling of our bedroom. It was the master bedroom we had just made perfect, the only truly finished room in the house. We looked at each other. Hand in hand, we walked back up the hill together.

"No more Lowes. No more Home Depot," I said with a smile.

"We can do all that traveling we said we would someday do," my husband added.

"We'll see our kids more, our grandchildren." I looked over to see our kids smiling.

"But we might need to keep just a few small tools for

emergencies," my husband said.

~~~~

A young couple bought the property. It was the land and the fishpond and glider swing that sold them. They had the house bulldozed down. They started anew on the same spot, adding a basement, but not before having the conjoined twins turned into stumps. The oaks never saw it coming. It pissed my husband off to see all that firewood go to waste. The new owners didn't need it. They were having gas fireplaces installed, along with a heat pump.

There was a smaller oak that stood off not too far from where the twin oaks once stood. It was the product of their parent's incestuous relationship. We surmised its acorn didn't fall too far from the tree.

Epilogue

The Carpenters spent their retirement traveling around in their motor home, visiting all fifty states except for Hawaii. One day, they hope to fly there. They spent their days having the sex they only dreamed of, reaching those orgasms that lay in wait. Before, they were always too tired from the house projects.

When they were not exploring America, they could be found parked in one of their three children's driveways. They lectured their grandchildren they needed to get away from the video games and play outside in the woods and in the creeks. The grandchildren gave them odd looks. Strangely, their own kids were now receptive to the idea and told their children how great life used to be. The Carpenters gave their children odd looks.

Sometimes when in the vicinity, they drove their motor coach back to check on things where their house used to stand. They told the young couple who lived there now that they were there to visit the Koi. After all, they took the trouble to name them. The new house owners gave them an ill-at-ease look every time they came, but the Carpenters just shrugged it off.

The house that stood there now was one of those brick mansions. They walked away up the newly paved shiny tarmac. It replaced their own gravel road, winding all the way to the new two-story brick. When they got to the door of their motor coach, Chris said to his wife, "Did you hear someone laughing?"

His wife gave him a knowing look. "Yes, it was the oak tree, the one they left standing."

"Should we warn them?" he asked.

"They already think we're insane."

The Carpenters never parked their motor home under oak trees. Nor, did they eat Oreos. On their travels, they sometimes drove past houses with an air of familiarity. They looked at each other, laughing and said in unison, "Fixer upper!"

Conversations in a Coffee House

HIS CLOTHES CAME straight from the racks of Goodwill—dingy camel jacket, dark faded black pants dropping in rolls atop well-worn sneakers, and a plaid shirt topped off with a wide paisley print tie. The tie must have been in the Goodwill shop for a good while. My college days were long over. Maybe this was the new chic, but somehow I didn't think so.

Both my husband and I watched, in a nonchalant manner, as we sipped our drinks. Much had changed. Yet little had changed. We were at the coffee bar in my old college town, except we had no coffee bar when I went to school—no lattes, no frappes, no espressos. In fact, we sat where the small town's theater used to be. One screen. Now, there was a new one down the road, ten screens. Okay, some things do change.

The theater seats had been removed to make way for book shelves, the town's only bookstore. The only bookstore when I went to school here had been the college bookstore.

We sipped our drinks, looking around at the pottery, all hand-thrown. This town was always a big pottery town. I took pottery classes when I was here. The art students had to be the wildest on campus. Although I was an art student, I was the anomaly. Still, I had the long hair, bell bottom jeans that only got washed once a week, and the halter top that gave the semblance of fitting in. And yet, even though I was the only one in the group of long-haired art freaks who hadn't smoked pot, I was still the only one who had a clue what the middle-school aged kid thought he could purchase from us when he approached us lingering on the steps of the Chicago Art Museum while awaiting the doors to open. Maybe that was because I was the only one who didn't have a pot hangover. I looked back over at the guy in the coffee shop. No, he didn't fit in.

"So, this was a theater when you went to college here?" my husband asked, breaking my trance.

"Yeah, I saw *American Graffiti* here. I saw it nine times." Why that particular memory popped in my head, I don't know.

"Nine times? Here?"

"No, I think three here."

"Why nine? Did you have the hots for Richard Dreyfuss?" He laughed.

"No, I think because I saw it three times I thought I had to set some kind of record. Well, maybe a little."

"What?"

"Maybe I had the hots for Richard Dreyfuss a little. If you haven't noticed I go for the offbeat, intellectual type." He smiled, pushing his glasses back up his nose. I looked back over at the weird guy. I would have probably been attracted to him back in the day.

"The first time I saw it I think everyone in the school was at the theater. Okay, that's an exaggeration. The theater could hardly hold everyone in the school."

Of course my husband had to bring up Ron Howard. He had once escorted him and his wife, and the ones who played Ralph Malph and Potsie with their wives around San Antonio. It was back in his younger days when he worked for a hotel there, long before we met. Although I was big on *American Graffiti*, I never got into *Happy Days*. Life was too busy then. I was winding up college and starting my first marriage.

"Did you have a date?" he asked.

"Yeah, three of them, or maybe just two. I probably went with girls on the other nights. I can only remember the first time in detail. It stood out."

"When did *American Graffiti* come out?" he asked.

I pulled out my iPhone to make sure. "1973." While perusing, I looked up *Happy Days*. It started in 1974 and ran for ten years. I would have been having my first child in that time slot. My husband would have moved on to another job, driving illegal aliens across the border. He lived a more rounded life than me, but then there was more opportunity in San Antonio.

"I was twelve then, and living in Belgium." My husband sometimes reminded me that he was younger.

"Okay, then," I said. "So that would make me twenty at the time. The guy I had a date with was a Vietnam vet. He was twenty-six, and at the time, he seemed ancient. Do I seem ancient to you?"

He smiled. "No, you look like you're in your thirties. I'm the one who looks old." He ran his fingers through his sparse gray hair.

"So, when are you going to shave off that beard?" The beard made him look older. "You could pass for a professor here."

The guy with the wide tie, who I might have been desperate enough to date back in the day, set his textbook on the coffee table and made his way from the overstuffed couch up to the counter. He stood behind two girls who were waiting in line. He asked what one of them was majoring in. I didn't hear her answer but heard his response, an elongated, *Nice*. *Nice* must have replaced *Cool*.

He stood in repose for perhaps a full moment before making another comment. The girl was politely talking to him, her friend standing to her side, before walking off to the other end of the counter to await their drinks, even though they could have gotten their drinks where they stood. He stood in their wake for a few moments, conceivably pondering his next move, before making his way over to them, yet keeping a safe distance. He looked in their direction. "There's a *Seller's* movie playing this weekend." His voice was loud, maybe to compensate for the five foot distance between them. They ignored him.

He stood there another moment in thoughtful repose before saying in a pronounced voice, "It was nice chatting with you." He made his way back to the overstuffed couch. The rejection didn't seem to deter him. He looked around for his next conquest.

"He's autistic. I heard him tell someone when I came back from the restroom," my husband said. "Tell me about the vet," my husband said, changing the subject. I jerked my head back in his direction.

"I kind of feel sorry for him but am fascinated and admire him at the same time," I said.

"The vet," he reminded.

I looked around. "Funny how everything changes, but there are still remnants of the past. Like, you can still tell this building was a theater. They didn't change much. The restrooms are pretty much the same. It seems to be in vogue for coffee houses to have sub-par restrooms. Most all the stores on the street have changed. The pizza restaurant across the street was here when I went to school. There was another pizza place down about two doors from it. Once, I was there, with a date, the guy who turned out to be my first husband, and we saw the waitress drink the overflow of a soft drink before taking it out to a customer. Never ate there again. It went out of business, needless to say. But the other one is still in business. It's probably the only restaurant in this whole town that's still here. I guess it was like the Starbucks of its day, in that you went up to the bar to order and gave them a name. My roommate always gave them a fake name. I remember I took my cup back up to get another drink. The man announced over the loud speaker, which is what they used to call out the fake names to come and get their orders, that bringing your same cup up was unsanitary. Shortly after I went back to sit down, some girls jumped up screaming because a mouse ran across the floor. Karma."

"Did you ever use a fake name?"

"Have you ever seen me use a fake name?" I retorted.

He laughed. "No, that's why I wondered if you might have back then."

"But I'll put using a fake name on my bucket list. Considering how old *American Graffiti* is I guess I'm running out of time. Anyway, that movie really had an effect on everyone."

"You didn't answer my question about the vet."

"My date, the old guy, the vet, wanted to take me to a nice restaurant after the movie. But everyone was going to the local drive-in restaurant. There was a lot of mooning. Everyone was reliving what they saw on the movie screen that night. But he wanted to eat inside. You just don't understand what is happening here, do you?" I said. "Don't you want to be involved in the experience?"

"So you ate outside," my husband asked.

"No, we ate inside. He wasn't as flexible as you are. He had to write a check for the meal. You know, back when we still used checks. For that, we had to go inside. He ordered spaghetti."

"You remember what he ordered? What did you order?"

"That I don't remember. Guys have this thing about spaghetti, don't they? You love spaghetti. My ex loved spaghetti. I've never known a guy to turn down spaghetti."

"So, did you moon?" He had an expectant look in his eye like I might have something as glamorous as moving illegal aliens across the border in my past.

"Have you ever mooned?" I whipped back at him.

"No."

"We are two peas in a pod, then aren't we?" At least in this part of life, I thought.

"Except you're not crazy about spaghetti. Is mooning on your bucket list?"

"No. And, you know I have no bucket list. If I had the butt I had back then it would be. If I had the body I had back then, a nude beach would be on my bucket list, if I did have one, not mooning."

"Your body's nice," he said. Did I hear a silence before he made that statement?

"You're a liar." There was no pause. "I have the kind of butt that inebriated people at a party might mistake for a side table and set their drinks on. How come no one ever invites us to parties?"

"I guess we're boring," he said. "I don't know, but you could dress like these college girls do now."

"With the midriffs hanging over?" I asked, with a slight raise of my eyebrows.

"Sure," he said. There was no pause this time. It was the espresso talking. I was sure of it.

"I don't think so. There's a big difference between young flab and old flab?" Out of the corner of my eye, I saw the guy getting ready to make a move.

"Streaking started when I was here," I said.

"And, I know you didn't do that either."

"No, but if I could go back in time, I think I would. A girl I took art classes with streaked. You would expect it to be the art students who streaked, right? I thought she was so beautiful. Her face was beautiful. She and her boyfriend didn't match at all. He was the Woody Allen type, at least in looks. I think they fought a lot, too. I think he may have hit her. There were rumors. I saw her in the shower once. I hated those dorm showers, no curtains. She had a great body, too. I hope she didn't end up with him."

"Did she have bruises?"

"I don't think so. I just glimpsed. Do you think I looked that long?"

He laughed. "I don't know."

"Are you surprised I have stories, too?"

"What do you mean?"

"You know, all that stuff you told me about your days working in the shoe store and as a cable guy. I honestly think you made most of that stuff up. And there was the police arrest you told me about. Anyway, she streaked with her boyfriend."

"The Woody Allen one?"

"Yeah."

My husband looked like he had swallowed something sour.

"She was like Lady Godiva. She had long black hair, at least long enough to cover her breasts. They ran through campus, through the crowded dark streets, holding hands. It was a blur. Wouldn't it have been so cool if they had been on a horse? Or groovy. We said groovy back then. Do they even say cool now?

"Anyway, streaking was new. They didn't really know how to handle it. I think the rule was just to let it run its course. The campus police were under explicit instructions only to monitor the situation. That's what I heard. But things got kind of wild that night. Accidentally, they cornered the couple inside the guy's dorm—right out of the dark streets into the dorm under those bright fluorescent lights like deer frozen in headlights. Both the cops and the couple."

"What happened then?"

"Everyone was outside. They weren't letting anyone in the dorm. I think the whole crowd kind of went silent. Someone eventually gave them blankets, and they left."

"So, that was your college streaking experience?"

"No, there's more. It gets better."

"Now I think you're going to make something up."

"Do you want me to tell you or not?" I said.

He took a drink of his espresso. "Yes."

The loner guy was making his way toward a bar stool. He sat next to a guy who had just ordered. "Do you know who my favorite entrepreneur is?" he asked the guy in the seat next to him. Whether the guy said yea or nay, the loner guy proceeded to tell him because he wasn't one to be deterred by lack of interest in his opinions. "I like Steve Jobs." Then he went on to explain to him who Steve Jobs was. The guy next to him might have murmured he's dead or something like that. Then the loner guy said, "I also like Bill Gates."

I directed my attention back to my husband. "The main streakers were coming down the main thoroughfare that ran through the dorms in different groups. The couple that ended up inside the dorm just got sidetracked."

"Probably nervous," my husband said.

"Yes, probably. Anyway, the next group came, I think all guys. I can't remember. There could have been a girl in there, but I'm not sure. Everyone thought it was over with. The crowd started breaking up. My date and I headed over toward one of the freshman dorms, actually, the one I stayed in as a freshman."

"Date? The vet?"

"No, a different guy. There are some stories there, too, but another time if you want to hear. So, we are out on the lawn, and I wanted some gum. I said I would wait outside on the lawn if he would go in and get me some from the vending machine. So, I'm standing out there at the corner of the building. There is a white picket fence next to me. A guy, another streaker, all by himself, jumps the fence, knocking me down. He is on the ground, too— legs spread apart with only tennis shoes on. They were orange with black trim."

"You looked at his tennis shoes?"

"No, I'm just kidding. I think they were white, but I don't know. We were like mannequins—he sprawled on the ground, me standing above him. He seemed scared out of his wits. I didn't think it was cold, but I guess if you were naked it might have been. I guess that would explain it."

My husband burst out laughing.

"My date was walking back about then. He pulled me off the ground. The guy got up and ran on. It all happened so fast but was still like one of those slow motion things, if you know what I mean. My date said, 'Guess you got your eyes full,' or something to that effect. I said, 'Not really.' He laughed, too, like you."

"Weren't you used to nude people? I mean you majored in art."

"Why would that make me used to nude people? I didn't have all that European experience that you did, going to nude beaches and all."

"I was twelve, you know, when I lived in Europe. Didn't you use nude models in art class?"

"No. They wore bathing suits. Nude models came after I went to school here, many years later. This is a conservative town, after all. You do know this is the Bible belt, don't you? The closest to nude was an end of the year assignment. This one guy did a life-size drawing of himself with only a t-shirt on. It's pretty bad when even the professor blushes. His last name was Key. In math class, he just put his last name on the final exam, and the graduate assistant used it to grade all the papers by. He did model for figure drawing some. There was this one girl. She was a great model. I wonder whatever happened to her. I helped her with one of her classes. In return she came over to the dorm and posed for me. She started talking about Rick."

"Your ex?"

"Yes. She didn't like him at all."

"Were you dating him then?"

"Yes, but I had just started. I let her talk. Didn't say anything. Then suddenly, she asked me who I was dating. Of course, she was embarrassed. I should have heeded her advice. Maybe I would have been with you sooner. But then, I would have had to wait. After all, you are younger."

97

"I'm glad you're with me now. Do you want anything else before we go home? Do you need to stop at the store?"

The loner guy walked by our table. He started asking a girl what her major was. She was standing next to her boyfriend. I didn't hear what she said, but the loner guy said in the same elongated fashion, "Nice."

"Hmm, I guess we could rent a movie," I said.

"How about *American Graffiti*? You could break your former record. Maybe we could pick up some pasta and marinara sauce."

"In other words, spaghetti. Yeah, that would be fine. We're boring, aren't we? Do you think there is still time for us?"

"Do you want to go to France to a nude beach on vacation?"

"I don't know. Maybe. Do AARP rates apply abroad?"

"So, if you could go back in time, would you streak?"

"If I could go back in time, I would study harder, and yeah, streak, too, if you could go back in time and streak with me."

"A twelve year old with a twenty year old. That would be weird."

"If we had the power to go back in time, we would pump your age up a bit or mine back."

"And we would go to the theater together and see *American Graffiti*. And moon each other."

"Are there any drive-in restaurants left?"

"Do you mean we practice first?"

"Maybe....work our way up to the nude beach."

"You know we'd be arrested."

"Yes, but you have experience with that."

"Hey, that was one time at a concert. Just happened to be sitting next to the wrong people. Anyway, you don't get arrested for mooning."

"But, I bet people would take pictures with their phones. We would go viral on Facebook. People would cringe at the sight, but still they wouldn't be able to look away."

"Yeah, maybe go on the Oprah Show. Then we'd get a free French nude beach vacation."

"Oprah doesn't have a show anymore. She hasn't had one for several years, at least not the kind where she gives away cars."

"Oh." He hesitated for a moment. "You know, this whole thing is backwards."

"What do you mean?" I asked.

"It should be like *Benjamin Button*. We should be born old and work our way back to being a baby. Then we'd have enough nerve and the bodies to do all this stuff in our old age—or young age."

"Yeah, true. Do you just want to see if *Benjamin Button* is on Netflix tonight?"

"Okay, or maybe a Peter Sellers movie."

"We could make popcorn."

"Are you ready to go?"

"Sure."

"Okay. Need to go to the restroom first."

"Again?"

"Yes. Be right back."

I looked back over at the guy. *He is getting up from the couch once again. Is he coming toward me? No, can't be. Yes, he is. He stands next to my table.* "So, you went to school here?" he asked. *Oh my god, has he has been listening to our conversation?*

"Yes," I said.

"What did you major in?" he asked.

"Art," I said.

"Niiiiiice."

Master of the Stacks

I GREW UP hearing *shh* all my life. My mom worked in a library, the university library, to be exact. She was a single parent, and because she couldn't afford a babysitter for me, I spent a lot of time in the library. I grew up with my nose stuck in books. We've all heard about the stacks. Some may be exaggerated, but a lot of it's true. I learned about sex in the stacks, some of it from books, but most of it from what I spied hiding in dark corners. I was smaller than most boys my age.

My sex education ended abruptly, when one night (my mom worked the night shift) an over enthusiastic janitor found me hiding in a cubbyhole. I was holding a used condom and an almost obliterated copy of *The Joy of Sex*. I was ten. I didn't mind, though. By that time, I pretty much had the physical aspects of the sexual act down. If I had gone to Sunday school, I might have thanked God for the experience. I did—under my breath. The janitor shook his head in a reproving manner, all the while with a giant grin. The man was yin and yang. As far as the emotional implications of sex went, I didn't have a clue. As I said, I was ten.

I'll never forget the look on my mom's face—one of shame and embarrassment, as she stood there frozen with an ashen face,

100

before taking my hand and walking with her head down while dragging me out of the library. It proved to be a blessing in disguise. My misdemeanor got her promoted to the day shift. Needless to say, it was a very long time before I was allowed to venture into the stacks again.

After this incident, all books I looked at had to first pass the scrutinizing eye of my mom. I also noticed after the occurrence, my mom's own taste in books had transitioned from mystery and romance novels to parenting books.

I went through various phases in subject matter. As a toddler, it was anything trains. In middle school, it was mysteries. I read every Hardy Boy book there was. By high school, I had moved to computers, not manuals, but the real thing. I was your typical nerd, braces and all. I wasn't the type of nerd that got crammed into a locker by the jocks. No, they wouldn't do that. I had computer skills, the kind that could get them into adult sites they normally couldn't get in to themselves. Myself, I was immune to porn. I had already seen it in the stacks. I was partial to the real thing. Not that I had experienced the real thing.

The real thing was Jennifer Josephine Roberts, Jenny Jo, for short. The problem was that Jenny Jo didn't know I existed. She was a cheerleader, totally out of a pimply faced nerd's league. But, I believed in miracles and preparation. I would be prepared for the day that Jenny Jo would know I co-existed with her on earth.

So, I went back to books. I studied what women wanted. A library is a great place. I could have written a thesis. Sadly, my four years of research on this subject matter only brought me to the realization that Jenny Jo didn't want me. Maybe my thesis should have been more along the line of how to make women *know* you exist at all.

After high school, I continued my studies during the summer. Maybe it was growing up in a library, but I found almost everything I encountered one big pool of information. I got a job in a health food store. Everyone came in with questions. What should I use for this, or what should I take for this condition? I studied up on vitamin supplements, herbs and bulking up.

There were a lot of bulking up questions. Still struggling with the remnants of being a scrawny, pimply faced kid, I knew their pain. By summer's end, I had shed my braces, cleared up my acne with apple cider vinegar, and had become a stud muffin. I also had a growth spurt of three inches. Maybe it was the vitamins or protein drinks. Working there, I got a lot of protein drinks for free. Or, maybe I was just due. I didn't know.

After a while, I ditched the apple cider vinegar. Girls didn't like the smell, although they were appreciative when I recommended they might use it as a rinse for their hair. I was full of little tidbits like that, stuff I had learned from working in the health food store and from the library. At one point, I had thought about writing my own book. I got as far as ten pages.

After summer's end, I enrolled in the same university where my mother worked. I got a student work study in the library, not on the same floor as my mom. That would have been disastrous to my new stud muffin appeal. I became master of the stacks. That ended when the same janitor caught me bare butt with a freshman in a larger cubbyhole. I was a senior by then. The freshman was a junior varsity cheerleader. It was something I needed to prove to myself. The janitor, once again, merely shook his head and smiled. The cheerleader said he was creepy. I looked over my shoulder as we were leaving to see him giving me a thumbs-up.

I graduated with a degree in library science. What does one do with a degree in library science? Fortunately, I had a minor in computer coding as well. I would spend a good deal of the remainder of my life in a cubicle. I still read a lot.

A couple of years went by. My trips to the gym became fewer, and my six-pack abs all but withered away. I dated around but nothing steady. With all the reading and sitting in front of a computer, my eyesight faded as well. A trip to the optometrist was in order.

In the waiting room, I met the most beautiful girl. She had long dark hair and even darker brown eyes, deeply set behind black oval frames. Her name was Cheri. My degree in library science finally paid off. It just so happened that she, too, had a degree in library science. We had something to talk about. Her job was archiving rare documents. She was also into yoga and health supplements, also right up my alley. If I were a religious dude, I would have praised God at that moment. Under my breath, I did.

I started going back to the gym. Some of the historical documents she was in charge of archiving were on the Kama Sutra. We both removed our glasses and studied Kama Sutra. Within a year, we were married. We spent our honeymoon in India.

After that, life settled down for us. My visits to the gym became fewer. Cheri fell behind on her yoga. It was nearly impossible with three kids. During the first pregnancy, we checked out every parenting book that was in the library. My mom was a great help in that area.

Cheri's parents were always traveling. Cheri, like me, was an only child. Her parents were the do-gooders of the world. They always had a cause. Growing up with one parent, it was just a struggle to get by. I'm not complaining. My mother poured out enough love for two parents. Cheri's parents dispensed a love that fell more along the lines of practicality.

Cheri's parents liked me well enough. They admired ambition. Working my way through college counted as ambition. Also, the novel I told them I had on the back burner didn't hurt either. I never got further than the ten pages, but I omitted that fact. They insisted I refer to them as Mom and Dad. It felt awkward. I never knew my own father. My mother refused to talk about him. I always thought I must have been conceived in the stacks. In looking back, it was written all over her face on the day the janitor caught me. Something I sensed.

I was determined to be a good father, a good husband. I was reading all the books I could on the subject matter during my down time at work. I figured out being a good husband and father just meant to be there for them—and for Cheri. I did my best.

Overall, we had a good marriage. The kids grew up and went off to college. Cheri's parents helped with that.

My mom retired, in a manner of speaking. Retirement didn't stop her from going to the library every day. She took our kids, the grandkids, every chance she got. The only rule was no stacks.

Then my mom got cancer. She moved in with us. I took a leave of absence from work. By this time, our oldest, Karen, was out of college and married. She was the closest to my mom. Karen came by every day. She spoon-fed her grandmother; that is when my mom would eat. My mom never did have much meat on her bones. She got most of her sustenance from books. She was all about stories. She always said, "The world is made up of stories."

She was almost down to the skeletal frame before losing all taste for food. That is what happens in advanced cancer. I tried all the stuff I learned at the health food store for her, but my mom wasn't much on vitamins or herbal formulas. The hospice workers who came by, daily now, frowned on it as well. So, Karen and I did our best to get the Ensure they provided down her.

My mom started seeing people, people who weren't there. Cheri said she already had one foot in the next world. Cheri was up on all of that. Cheri read all the Wayne Dyer and Deepak Chopra books ever published. She was big on spirituality.

Mom saw her grandmother whom she had been particularly close to. People from her past, now deceased, would come and go, the same as any other visitor. She had plenty of living visitors. She had made many friends over the years from working at the university library. Sometimes the house seemed like Grand Central Station. On the bright side, they brought food, food that my mom wouldn't eat. We rarely cooked for the last three months of my mom's life. That is how long she lasted.

My mom seemed immune to pain. We were all thankful for that. There was no morphine involved. I knew that was prevalent in most of these cases. The only pain she had was what I may have inflicted on her over the years. Time was drawing short. I wanted to know about my father. She was reluctant but said in a weakened voice, "Yes, you have a right to know."

I held her boney hand and propped her up in the hospital bed that had taken over our living room. Mom liked to look out the window. In the distance, you could see the spire that sat atop of the library. She stared for hours at that spire. I put a wet sponge to her mouth. Slowly, she moved her lips, "That's where it happened." There was a slight smile on her face and a warmth in her eyes.

"What happened, Mom?"

She continued in her weakened voice, "Where you were conceived."

The spire rose above the section known as the stacks. I thought she might be remembering my indiscretions, or she could be delusional again. I held the cup for her as she did her best to drink some water using the straw. I wiped away the dribble on her chin, where gray bristly hairs sprouted. The one thing that caused her pain was when Cheri plucked them. So Cheri stopped. It was kind of useless now anyway.

Mom gazed out the window. "He was a rare book dealer. I helped him with research using the microfilm machine. That's what we had before computers."

"Mom, are you saying this book dealer was my father?"

"Yes. I was just a student at the time. He was older. Day after day, he came by, and day after day I helped him. We met there. He told me later that he was married. He said that his wife didn't care much for books, rarely ever picked up a magazine."

Even after all this time of not having a father figure in my life, this news shook me to the core. Outwardly, I remained calm. The last three months had taught me a lot. One never knew how strong one was until tested. My mother's illness had tested me in so many different ways. I did things I never thought I could do. There was a part of me that was a rock of Gibraltar, and another part of me that could crumble at any moment. The crumbling moment I would put aside until after my mother's funeral. I couldn't let her see me fall apart.

There was always a part of me that wanted to know about my father. Still there was a part of me that said don't stir up trouble. I sat holding my mother's hand, feeling the trouble coming on. My mind was flitting all over the place. Did I have half-brothers or half-sisters out there? Was my father still alive? I waited for my mom to say more. Sometimes in mid-sentence, she would just close her eyes and doze off for a bit. She was doing that a lot now. Revealing this sapped what little strength she had. It was sapping mine as well. I longed for Cheri by my side, but she was at work. I was glad Karen wasn't here. This moment was meant for my mom and me. There were no visitors, no hospice workers, only the two of us. It was just like when I was a kid.

She opened her eyes once again. They say you can see a person's soul in their eyes. The soul in my mom's eyes had packed its suitcases. A watery blur replaced vitality. The past three months had taught me more about life than I had ever learned from reading books. The only thing close to this experience was looking at each of my three children after they were born. That was a funny comparison. There was something similar in new life coming into the world and old life departing it.

Her last words were my father's name and the town he lived in. My mother had kept up with him. His name was Michael. My name was Michael. The last words on my mom's breath were, "Michael Burns, Michael." She said his name and then my name. I'm glad it was my name that she spoke last. After saying it, she closed her blank eyes. Before she closed them, they were looking straight ahead, at the spire, not at me. I held her hand for a while longer, and a tear rolled down my cheek.

I heard the front door open. It was Cheri coming home from work. She came over and took my other hand. Then she called hospice. We had been drilled on what to do. In less than half an hour, they appeared. Pills were flushed down the commode. Paperwork was started. The official time of death was when they took the non-existent pulse and filled out the paperwork, but that wasn't real. I had glanced over at the clock at the fateful moment when my mother passed and for the first time in my life spoke my father's name. It was 4:33 P.M. I will always remember that.

The kids came by and waited with us. The funeral home people came shortly after and took away the body. We sat in silence for the most part for a couple of hours. All the preparation still didn't prepare you. I broke the silence. "Michael Burns is my father, your grandfather." The kids looked at me. We hugged. "We will talk tomorrow," I said.

Cheri, the kids, and I carried out my mother's wish. We spread her ashes on the library lawn, 433 Burns Avenue.

About two months after the funeral, I worked up the nerve to check out my dad. I had waited too late. He had died a day after my mother had. If I had been a religious man, I would have questioned God on this coincidence. I did—under my breath.

His son had inherited his used bookshop. I went in and browsed, but I didn't buy anything. I made some small talk with the son. He seemed like a nice enough fellow. I didn't see any reason to disrupt his life. I walked out and looked at the sky. I was

amazed at how beautiful the day was. I called Cheri and asked
her to meet me at the park. I will never forget that day. We sat on
the park bench and talked about the mysteries of life. On the
way home, we bought an expensive bottle of wine and made love
until the wee hours of the morning.

Time passed. All the kids married, Karen, twice. We went
through the usual struggles. We had our share of joys. Cheri and
I became grandparents a total of six times, four boys, and two
girls.

Not too long after retirement, while mowing the lawn, I felt a
pain in my chest. Cheri found me on the ground. I kept telling
her not to cry, but she couldn't hear me. I watched as people
brought food to the house. I watched the grandchildren playing
in the yard, the same spot where I took my last breath. I watched
my children and their spouses comforting Cheri.

I floated toward a light. I saw my mom, but she wasn't in
physical form. I wasn't in physical form. I wanted to tell Cheri
what it was like, but that was impossible.

The next thing I knew, I was in this massive celestial
dimension. Points of light were busily perusing information. My
mom told me, not in a physical voice, mind you, but through
what one on earth might call telepathy, "It's called the Akash. It's
where the Akashic records are kept."

"The Akash?" I inquired.

"Yes, it's a record of anything and everything that ever
happened, plus all the possibilities of what could have happened,
and have yet to happen. It makes our poor excuse for a library on
earth pathetic."

I was in awe. Just then, another point of light approached.

My mom addressed me. "Michael, we go by different names
here. I will explain that later, but for now, meet your father."

A phantom part of me reached out a hand to shake where
there was none. The point of light conveyed, "I was Michael
Burns in the life we undertook together."

"The life?" I inquired again. It was all so overwhelming, but at
the same time, a wave of peace flooded every aspect of my being.

This point of light that was once a physical being on earth, and also my biological father, said, "Yes, we all have many lives. You haven't had your review yet. You will understand then. For instance, my name was Burns on this last earth life. I am using last life purely as a reference. Everything happens simultaneously. It's all one big moment. There is no time. Time is an earth illusion. There are so many possibilities. But, as I was saying, my name was Burns. You will find the celestial powers have a sense of humor. It is one of those karmic things. There was a time in earth's history when I burned books. To make up for that negative karma, I became a rare book dealer in the life I knew your mother. And now, well, I'm assigned to the Akashic records. Burning books is a pretty big transgression."

I looked around and saw the souls watching multi-dimensional depictions, a more advanced form of motion pictures. My mom spoke, and I use that term loosely, "They are reviewing past lives, examining their mistakes and triumphs, and planning for future lives. You will find you have all knowledge, all wisdom at your command. You only have to ask. The world is made up of stories. They are all here."

I was in heaven.

Man's Best Friend

"SURPRISE!" BERNIE SAID as he removed his hands from Doris's eyes.

"An amusement park?" she gasped, trying not to show disappointment, while clutching her bag.

"Not just any amusement park. The Jungle Park. Action and adventure for the whole family, that's what the brochure said."

"But Bernie, there is just the two of us. And, we are not a family." A slight whimper emerged into the air, and Doris covered her bag with her hands. "This is our third date, and we're a little past the family stage." Doris blushed.

"Did you hear something?" Bernie asked.

"No," Doris looked around as if to discover the sound he thought he had heard.

"Oh well, probably nothing. Do you want a piece of candy?"

"No."

"Are you sure? It's butterscotch."

"Butterscotch? No." Another whimper. Doris reached her right hand into her bag, pretending to look for something.

"Are you sure you didn't hear anything?" Bernie looked around.

"I hear lots of noise, Bernie. After all, we are standing at the

110

entrance of an amusement park."

"You're right. Oh, well. Probably nothing. Let's get in line for our tickets."

"The gates are certainly big and pearly white," Doris said, as she placed her right hand on top of her bag and held onto Bernie's arm with her left hand.

"By the way, what do you have in that thing? Sure is big."

"What?"

"Your bag. Sure is big. I know ladies carry big purses, but that one takes the cake."

"Nothing, just stuff."

"How about the roller coaster?" Bernie asked as they made their way through the gate.

"The rollercoaster?" Doris looked at him with a crinkled forehead.

"You'll be fine. I'll hold onto you extra tight. He gave her a squeeze. It'll be our first ride. The rest of them will be easy. What do you say? Let's go for it," he said with a pleading look in his eyes.

~~~~

Doris gripped one hand tightly around the front bar and the other one around her bag. "It sure is a long way down."

"Don't worry, Hon. I've got you." He snuggled closer putting his arm around her. "Whoa, what was that? Something moved. I felt something wet on my fingertip."

Grrr.

Bernie jumped back as far as the seat would let him. "You have a dog in that bag?"

"She's so small, Bernie." Doris asserted with a scared look. "I just got her last week. I couldn't leave her home by herself. Look at her. She's just a puppy."

Bernie looked at her and back at the dog's minute head peeking from the bag. "Oh, well, no harm. He's already here. Just keep him hidden. The ride is about to start. Don't want to get kicked off."

"She," Doris corrected, but they started moving forward into a descent, and a zillion screams drowned her voice.

"What?" Bernie shouted, with his arm wrapped around Doris and his hand hovering over her bag.

"The dog is a she. Her name is Buttercup." Doris tried to shout above the screams, but there was no use.

"What?" Bernie shouted.

Millions of shrill dog whistles. I think I'm going crazy. We're up so high. Don't they know I'm scared of heights? Why didn't she leave me home? Fill my food and water bowl, leave a few dog biscuits scattered around. Pop in a "Lassie" DVD? I would have been fine.

~~~~

"The jungle boats, let's head that way." Bernie grabbed her arm, taking off in a mad rush. "Push that dog back down into your bag. We don't want to get in trouble. What did you say his name was? Butterscotch?"

A herd of preschoolers ran by, talking and shouting all at once.

"Buttercup, and it's a she."

"What? I didn't hear you, Hon."

"Oh, never mind," she said, taking off after him, holding tightly onto her bag.

~~~~

"Be careful, now. Don't rock the boat," Bernie said.

What are those sounds? They are coming from that jungle next to the water. Water! Don't they know I can't swim? What do they think I am? A lab? I'm a Dachshund, for heaven sakes. Look at these paws. Do they think I could maneuver in the water with these? And these ears. I'll sink faster than an anvil. Oh, no. I remember my master saying pearly gates. I'm doomed.

That was a lion's roar. I know that sound. He's coming for the boat. I just know it. Dog overboard!

"Bernie," Doris screamed. "She's headed for the falls. Do something."

"What can I do? Butterscotch, Butterscotch!"

"She can't hear you. The waterfall— it's too noisy. And it's

Buttercup."

Is this what it feels like to die? I'm sinking, sinking. Everything is in slow motion. What is that sound? Is it the waterfall? No, I think it's the sound of OM. I'm going home. My life is flashing before my eyes. It's times like these I wish I were a cat.

I'm caught. Oh, no. My red kerchief is caught on a branch. Now, I'm not only going to drown, I'm going to choke as well. What was my master thinking?

What's that? The hand of God? No, it's Bernie. He's saving me. You're all wet, Bernie.

"Come on, Butterscotch, I've got you. You'll be fine."

It's Buttercup, Bernie. Oh, never mind. You're my best friend, Bernie. In fact, you're my hero.

"Now where is the doorway out of here?" Bernie scratched his drenched thinning hair with one hand, while grasping onto Buttercup firmly with the other.

Oh, Bernie, I'm sorry. I bet that watch is ruined. What was that sound? A tiger, I'm sure of it. Are we lost, Bernie? I need to pee. Is that a real tree? It looks fake. The grass, it looks like AstroTurf. I'm sure of it. Is this even a real jungle, Bernie? It doesn't smell like a real jungle. I know. I've got a good sniffer.

"Do you want a piece of candy? It's butterscotch, Butterscotch. No, I don't suppose so. You might choke."

We're lost in the jungle, and you're worried about me choking on a piece of candy? Bernie, did you just throw that wrapper on the ground? That's littering. We are so going to get in trouble. Oh, no. What was I thinking? Hansel and Gretel, right? You're leaving candy wrappers, so we won't go in circles. Smart thinking, Bernie. You're my hero.

I see light, Bernie. You saved the day. You saved my life, again. You're my hero and my best friend.

"Sir, did you know you are not supposed to bring pets to the park? I'm afraid I'm going to have to ask you to leave."

~~~~

"Bernie, Bernie, are you okay? And my precious little Buttercup," Doris said. as she took the wet dog from Bernie's arms. "Are you going to be all right?"

Butterscotch, Master. I've changed my name to Butterscotch. We're going to be such a great family.

When in Paris

WE'RE LOST. THE hotel is nowhere in sight, not even a familiar landmark, not even the Eiffel Tower. No GPS. Turning on the cell would be too expensive. I was one of the last holdouts in getting a cell phone. Not THE last. My husband still doesn't have one. I didn't want the dependence, the stress. He doesn't see the need. Now, I have one and can't use it because of the roaming fees.

The Paris trip that we put off for more than a decade has already gone over budget. A couple of Euros to the beggar on the street in exchange for directions did no good. He snatched up the offering saying "No English."

It's 10 P.M, and the streets have thinned out. My husband and I find ourselves in a residential neighborhood. A limo pulls up to an apartment building. A lady dressed to the nines gets out and rings a buzzer. "Do you think she's a high-class prostitute?" I whisper.

My feet ache. I estimate we have walked at least fifteen miles today. My husband is arguing that we should find the subway. But I insist on walking, as we tend to get lost on the subway as well. I would rather be lost out in the fresh air, where I can at least observe the nightlife of Paris.

We are getting a lot of fresh air. I think we are going in the wrong direction. An hour later, we find a large map erected on the wide sidewalk. Yes, we have completely gone in the opposite direction. It's eleven, and the streets have livened up and are lined with tables, all of them being used. Wine is flowing, and waiters are bringing out entrees.

"Who eats at eleven?" I ask my husband. My digestive track would never allow it. "Is anyone even home in this city?" I added. Mind you these are rhetorical questions, or at least my husband must think so, as he hasn't bothered to offer an opinion.

An hour later, at the stroke of midnight, we find ourselves on a street with expensive storefronts. None of the stores are open. I eye a camisole in the window, one hundred and fifty Euros on sale. We are definitely in the wrong neighborhood. A group of men and women, clad in the finest fashion, are coming out of one of the buildings, a huge, grand building that looks as though it could withstand a bomb attack, as is the case with most of the buildings here. They are laughing as one of them locks up. Is this when business deals are made, at midnight, the witching hour?

Across the street, a man and woman depart a jewelry store that is dark inside, all the while kissing. She admires the ring on her finger. He kisses her again and opens the door of his Jaguar, that is parked in front of the store, for her.

Another string of restaurants. I recognize the lady who got out of the limo. Hmm, she could have given us a lift. She is dining with a younger girl. They look alike. It must be her daughter.

We look up to see the Arch de Triomph. We estimate another three miles to our hotel. My husband squeezes my hand and bends down to kiss me and yanks me in the opposite direction toward a vacant table at an outside café. He orders a bottle of wine. Only one more day of this trip, and we are just now getting it.

Back at our hotel, we make love, the first time on our romantic getaway. The first light of Paris comes through the window. I say, "Cinderella would have saved herself a lot of trouble if only she had not been so rigid about that midnight thing." We close our eyes.

The Lost Moment

WAITERS, PIMPLY FACED skinny boys alongside men teetering just on the other side of the prime of their life, scurry about, meandering between crisp white tablecloths, dessert carts, and their patrons, all the center of their own universes, engaged in various modes of culinary pursuits, romantic liaisons and business deals. Conversations are low, almost whispered, as is the background music, which I recognize as Mozart. The whole scene exemplifies subtle elegance. Except for the slender vases of pink roses in the center of the tables, the theme is black and white. Women are in sleeveless black, tight fitting dresses and men, except for their seated positions, don't differ too much from those pouring their wine. It reminds me of the monochrome movies that I watched with my mom when I was a child, except this is the real world, and the people I observe are not as sleek and perfect as those I remember on the television screen.

I glance sideways at my bare arms, relishing in the fact they are still smooth and have some muscle tone. They aren't too tan. Nor are they translucent like those of the woman in the party seated before us. Eyes cushioned in blue veined faces like blue lined note paper peer at each other. Albinos come to mind. Is that term even politically correct anymore?

I probably would not even have known that term if I hadn't seen one while growing up, an albino that is. The word was strewn about the room in hushed whispers about a man who rode around on a bicycle throughout my small mid-western town. Pale eyelashes and eyebrows rose from his invisible skin like textured tapestry. That, along with his ubiquitous clothing, would have surely been dangerous on roads more heavily traveled. But, we lived in farm country where old pickup trucks and slow moving farm machinery were the norms. Everyone knew him. Everyone waved as they passed. "There's Red Ed," they would say, as they continued on with their business. He was called Red Ed because he dyed his hair red. The shiny blue of his bicycle, which he always kept polished, gleamed in the sun as a mirage emerging from the horizon as it came over a knoll we loosely defined as a hill. I know better now. I live in San Francisco.

As for the couple in the restaurant, I would have suspected at first glance, brother and sister, but switched my assumption to vampires out for a late bite when he wrapped his arm around her waist and with a familiar ease slipped his bony blue-veined hand bearing a ring similar to the one which Barnabas Collins wore on Dark Shadows, downwards on to her ample behind, the only part of her that exhibited any fat. I immediately adjust my momentary gaze toward her face to see her candy red lips curve upward. Their thick brilliance against the pale powdery flesh of her face lead me to believe it is more like dessert and champagne after the kill. I tilt my head and run my fingers through my mousy brown curls, looking up with a casual glance, all a ruse to cover up my contemplation of the couple. I see no blood dripping from his mouth, just a smile that says costly dental work.

We are seated. I lose track of the couple. Like a detective, I spy them at the far corner of the restaurant, in a cozy spot that says they want to be alone. Their location speaks volumes. It says the man had money to tip the maître d' for such a chosen table off the beaten path. From the looks of his tailored suit, he reeks of money, more than likely old money. Their conversation is serious. Not to be discovered gawking, I turn my own eyes toward my date.

We sit in the middle of the hustle and bustle. All roads lead to Rome. All aisles through the crowded, no table vacancy restaurant lead to us. I look up at my date. Or should I say boyfriend? After six months, it is time to drop the label of date and say boyfriend, or significant other, or whatever they are calling it these days. He has rattled on all night, chopped and stringy sentences, unsure of himself. He is out of place in this scene. Me, I can take it or leave it. I have a way of stepping outside of myself which makes my presence exude confidence. No one would ever know I grew up in a small mid-western town.

Our waiter is in training. I want to give him an old folk remedy that only mid-western girls such as myself would know for clearing up his acne but think better of it. A more established waiter is refilling the water glasses of the pale couple in the corner. I purposely move my chair so that I am sitting down on the side facing their direction. Except for one table, I have an unhampered view. As long as the older woman with the flabby arms retains her position, I have a clear view.

Andrew is my date. We will leave it at that. Even though physically we are in the advanced stages, emotionally I haven't been able to move forward. For some reason, that seems to escape Andrew. Perhaps instead of moving to San Francisco, I should have moved to New York or Los Angeles and taken up acting.

Andrew orders champagne. I fear the obvious, as I see him fumbling around in his pocket. This has happened before. It was also at a restaurant, a couple of weeks ago. It was a new trendy Japanese one.

We waited the second weekend of its opening. First nights or first weekends are always a hassle. Andrew had heard from his accounting firm that it was up and coming chic. Never trust accountants when it comes to restaurants. What Japanese restaurant doesn't serve pots of hot tea with spring rolls and seaweed salad? My dismay over that blunder ruined the mood. Nor did the significant perspiration odor coming from our young waiter set the background for romantic overtures. Early on, Andrew quit reaching in his coat pocket. The whole night was growing dismal as we waited beyond measure for our first course to arrive. Finally, a manager showed up at our table saying he would take over, as our own waiter quit midstream. I couldn't help but wonder if it was my alarm over no pot of jasmine that drove him to ditch his black uniform and head out the back door for a shower no doubt. I hope.

Tonight is different. Andrew is glowing. This restaurant is upscale. The odds are in his favor. Andrew is a big odds man. Aren't all accountants? The waiter returns. Is it my imagination or has he been off in the kitchen somewhere squeezing that pimple? No, it's just the lighting. I am just looking for things, something to complain about. Doesn't Andrew see that about me? I want to tell him that he is settling, but I'm too interested in the couple in the corner to cause a scene.

Andrew is a placeholder. He has been for the six months since I've known him. A placeholder for what or who, I don't know. I've been far too demanding when it comes to men. That is my mother's voice.

There has been a stream of Andrews left in my wake. They all moved on, married, started families. Maybe it's time I cave and settle too. Andrew is thirty-eight. I will be forty in another month. I've held my age well. The older lady with the flabby arms moves in toward her husband. She blocks my view. I've heard spinsters retain their youth. Spinster would be my mother's term. She says that is what I'm becoming.

The waiter stands solo at our table. His trainer has moved on. Perhaps he has graduated. Is that a small diploma I see sticking out of his pocket? No, it is his order pad. None of the other waiters use them, but then he lacks confidence. He struggles but pops the champagne lid. As he does, his accompanying fart harmonizes to a full falsetto with the sound of the cork popping and flying like a cannonball across the room. It heads in the opposite direction of the pale couple. Everyone else's eyes are either on us, our waiter, or in the direction of the cork. I can't help but smile. I don't indulge in laughing out loud as the tables next to us do. That would be rude and uncouth.

Andrew's face is red. I study it. His freckles have faded into the crimson. A heavy sigh escapes his thin lips. What would our children look like? Maybe cute at first. All children are. But they would morph into chips off the old blocks, plain and drab, when I filter in my own nothing that stands out looks, along with Andrew's receding hairline and beginnings of a potbelly. No, as a couple we definitely don't have what it would take in the gene pool to produce anything remarkable.

I look back toward the corner. The couple has drawn closer to each other, oblivious to what is happening in the center of the restaurant. He reaches his hand across the table and touches her cheek. Her thick mascaraed eyelashes gravitate downward as her red lips curve upward. Even in the dim light, I can see a touch of pink on her cheek. Andrew's own glow has evaporated. He removes his right hand from his jacket pocket. The waiter walks away, his shoes squeaking and sticking in the bubbly beneath his feet. Before his embarrassed exit off into the kitchen, he reaches down with the last remaining dignity he can muster and retrieves the cork.

A different waiter returns. His skin is clear. He is toting a new bottle of champagne and announces that our meal will be on the house. This decree does nothing to restore Andrew to his former nervous glory. The moment is gone. I excuse myself to go to the powder room. Instead, I find the waiter lurking in the back of the restaurant and say, "Thank you." His glum look changes to one of bewilderment. I walk back to my table with a feeling of victory. I order a rich, deep chocolate dessert. Even though it's on the house, Andrew passes on dessert. Unlike Andrew to pass up anything free. I sense he sees a pattern with me and waiters and blames me for our poor dining experiences. I notice the couple has left.

~~~~

Mid-week, I meet Andrew outside his office building for lunch. It was where we first met. He was insistent. He normally brown bags it during the week. We sit on a bench. Once again, he reaches into his pocket. I can clearly see the outline of a small box. He places his bag on the bench and begins to rise, adjusting his pants to allow room for what I can see only as one knee bending into a forward lunge. I stop him mid-stride. "Andrew, I wanted to tell you I will be moving." His face reminds me of that of the waiter, both glum and perplexed. "To New York," I add. Those words came out totally unexpected.

There was nothing else to say. I get up and walk away. As I walk, I think I give Andrew another six months, or maybe less. He already has the ring.

A block away I see the albino couple. What are the odds? I'm sure Andrew might have been able to tell me. She is wearing a bright red dress and shoes to match. He is in a white linen suit. They are arguing. He grabs her arm, but she pulls it free. They go in different directions, she up toward the designer shops, he off into the direction of the blazing sun. I watch as his white silhouette merges into the bright ball's fiery glow like a mirage. I hope he has sunscreen.

Lunch time has ended. I walk back toward the laboratory where I work, but I'm thinking of changing careers, one not so analytical.

The Red Geraniums

I WAKE TO a rippling stream and voices off in the distance. For a moment I forget the day before. I had run from early morning into the night, my heart pounding the whole way. I had only stopped once for water and only when I thought I had lost him.

The next time I stopped was from sheer exhaustion and from utter darkness. There were no stars or moon to guide me. But if I had heard even the slightest of sounds, a crunch of leaves, a heaviness of breath behind me, I would have found a way to continue through the blackness.

Only the sound of the water and my beating heart. Once, I thought I heard my name being called. I think I imagined it. Earlier there were coyotes and wolves, but their yelping ceased. I collapsed next to a tree. And now, I see the sun glimpsing through the trees. The warmth on my face feels as if my mama's hand is caressing me. I can feel her presence. I know I have done the right thing.

The bed of leaves I made for myself is damp, not with morning dew but from my sweat. I look down at my leg. The leaf poultice I had made before collapsing has fallen off during the night. The blood on my leg is dry. Nothing serious, just a briar patch I should have avoided, but I was too busy looking over my shoulder. Maybe he wasn't following me at all. Maybe it was my imagination.

I lay on the hard ground. Last night was the best sleep I ever remember. Not that I remember. But, that is good. Not even a dream. I am so used to dreams—or rather nightmares. I wore myself out. A loud growl from my mid-section. My stomach feels hollow. My last meal was dinner, the day before yesterday. I packed biscuits for my escape but in my fright, lost them somewhere along the way. Probably long gobbled up by those coyotes or wolves by now. I did hear them once during the night and jerked awake but went back to sleep in an instant. So tired. Their sounds couldn't even disrupt the slumber I so longed for. It was a relaxed sleep. No lying stiff in my bed with fear, hearing his snores from the other room, dreading the moment they stopped, recoiling from the sound of his footsteps growing louder as they approached. And the smell of wine on his breath, and the stubble of his beard as he climbed into my bed.

I rise from my bed of leaves, and my legs wobble. The side of my leg burns from the scratches of the briar patch. I look down to see the edge of my dress is torn, my best dress, the dress my mama made for me. I want to cry but don't. I have only two, the other being my work smock. I left that one behind. I wanted no remembrance of it.

This one is too tight. My mama gave it to me on my birthday, a little over a year ago, about a month before she fell sick. She said the blue matched the color of my eyes.

He never touched me when I wore the blue dress. I think because Mama made it. That is why he hid it from me, but I found it. And the cross, too. They were together. She meant for me to have it, I know. That is why I took it. I caress it between my fingers, the way my mama did. It gives me hope. I try to remember the prayer she taught me, but the words are lost to me. They'll come back to me when I'm calmer, I'm sure.

Hail, Mary! Full of grace,
The Lord is with thee,
Blessed…I can't remember.

The voices. There are more of them now. They are coming from the valley just over the knoll. Men. I don't want to encounter them. What choice do I have? I can't go back. I can't stay here. I'm so hungry. I gather my strength and courage. I feel Mother Mary with me. My mama told me Mother Mary would keep me safe. She even named me Mary.

There must be someone over the hill, a kind woman who might give me food. I must make myself presentable. I wash in the cold stream as best as I can. I gently remove the caked blood from my leg. I walk as I can no longer run. My legs are sore, and I'm weak from hunger. I look behind me. Only the woods. Nothing stirs. Only the sound of birds and the stream. A good sign.

I make my way up the small hill. When I reach the peak, I look down to see the grandest structure I have ever seen. A tall spire coming from a round dome reaches towards the heavens. The buildings attached to the building with the spire seem to go on forever. They are made of giant stones, the kind the men are moving. It is where the voices are coming from.

I sit on the hill, taking in the situation. Coming around the corner of one of the buildings, I see women in black flowing robes with large white collars and white caps. They walk in pairs. I count twelve. My mama taught me to count to one hundred and eight. It was the number in her rosary beads. I so wish I had them. I wanted to bring them. I looked but couldn't find them. Maybe he hid them. But I suspect he threw them away. My papa wasn't a religious man.

I watch the women walk around the building as they disappear one by one. They are nuns. My mama told me about them. They will help me. I am sure of it. Once again, I rise and make my way down toward the valley.

I approach the building. The men ignore me. Still, I tremble as

I walk past them. I spy one lone nun outside. She looks young, yet several years older than me. She stands before the grandest doors I have ever seen. I think these doors must be meant for giants. My mama told me fairy tales about giants. My papa would sometimes tell me stories as well, before he became different after my mama died.

The nun's habit is all white. I remember my mama using the word habit to describe what the nuns wore. She is tending some flowers. I learn later that they are geraniums. I think they are the most beautiful flowers I've ever seen.

I stand in the distance, my legs too weak to move forward. But it is mostly from fear. I've come this far. Now what do I do? I grasp onto the cross that hangs from my neck. In that instant, the nun looks up. She is also wearing a cross. I see her touch it. A tortured look is on her face. I'm sure the same look is on my own. She makes herself smile, and I can tell she is doing so to calm me. I try to smile back. She reaches out a hand. I feel saved. I rush toward her. I feel myself in her arms, and then a dizziness overtakes me and all goes black.

~~~~

I wake to hear faint sounds of children singing. All girls. I am relieved there are no male voices.

Frère Jacques, frère Jacques,
Dormez-vous? Dormez-vous?
Sonnez les matines! Sonnez les matines!
Ding, dang, dong. Ding, dang, dong.

The nun in the white habit peeks through the doorway. Although, she has a big smile on her face, I still jump up, startled. I'm sitting up in the narrow bed, one in a row of many. I want to count them, but she is speaking to me. "You slept for hours. I hope you are rested now. You must be starved. Lunch will be served soon. I came to help you freshen up."

128

I try to make words, but they don't come. I don't know what to say. I finally settle on, "Merci." She smiles again. I see her teeth are white like the clouds. I think of my own dull teeth I saw through my papa's shaving mirror.

I only thought to pack the biscuits which I lost. I didn't bring my toothbrush or hairbrush. I look down at my dress. It is dirty from my escape. I feel ashamed. My appearance must have been the reason for the tortured look I saw on her face when she first beheld me. Now, she just smiles with her beautiful white teeth and looks at me from the bluest of eyes. They remind me of the pond near our cottage, the cottage that is no longer mine.

Her face is calm and reassuring. Her cheeks are rosy. I remember my mama pinching hers to make them that way. But, somehow, I think the nun's are natural. I don't know what to think. I'm both frightened and relieved at the same time. And, I'm hungry, very hungry.

"My name is Mary," she says. "What's yours?"

My eyes widen. I say, "Mary," slowly, timidly. I hope she believes me. My mama would call this a sign. My mama believed in signs and miracles. My papa didn't. He said no miracles happened to save her life. He said it was all foolishness.

"Well, then, we will be great friends. We already have something in common," she says, placing her hand on my arm. I like its warmth.

"And blue eyes," I say, but after I say it, I think how stupid it sounds.

But she smiles and says, "Yes, and blue eyes."

I almost break into tears but hold back. My teeth chatter, and my lips quiver even though the summer air is warm. I have been fighting back the tears for days. I can no longer contain them. She holds me to her chest and says, "Now, now, it will be all right."

I want to believe her. I am both happy and sad. Happy that I escaped. Sad that I have such a miserable life, and they may feed me and send me on my way.

"I have nowhere to go," I blurt out between my sobs.

"It's okay. You are here. You don't need to go anywhere."

"Really?" I ask, my crying coming to a halt.

"Really. We will visit Mother Superior before lunch. So, let's make you presentable. She is the one who makes these decisions. Not me. I am just a novice."

"A novice?" I ask.

"Yes, a novice. In training to become a nun. It was my dream. I turned eighteen last month and started my discernment period."

I do not know what any of this means, but something inside me says this is what I want, too. I look at her, more tears welling up in my eyes.

"But don't worry. I've never seen her turn anyone away. She runs the orphanage." She squeezes my hand. "Now, let's get you cleaned up. We can't be late. Mother Superior frowns on lateness. And then, lunch. You must be starving."

"I am," I say, trying to muster a smile.

~~~~

"You must work while you are here," she says with a sternness in her voice, all the while looking deep into my eyes, studying me over, summing me up as if trying to determine whether I might be good grape or a bad grape, much the way my papa did at harvest time.

I almost blurt out that I am a good grape, but instead, I say, "I will work, whatever it takes. I can't go back home."

Her eyes flinch, and she stiffens. "I was of the understanding you had no home to go to. You have no mother, you said."

"No, Mademoiselle." I hold my eyes down.

"Mother Superior," Mary whispers to me.

"No, Mother Superior," I say, still holding my eyes down.

"You made no mention of a father," she says.

I hesitate. "No, Mother Superior." I sensed she knew I was lying. She heaved a heavy sigh.

"Mary, she will be your charge for the time being. Assign her kitchen duties and instruct her as to our schedule. We follow a strict schedule," she says directing her eyes back toward me. "And you must obey all of the rules. Mary will see you are settled in, child. You can begin your duties tomorrow."

"Oui, Mother Superior, merci."

Mary curtsied, and we exited the office. When she closed the door behind us, she said, "See, I told you it would be okay."

"Merci, Mary. I am so glad I found you."

~~~~

I enter the dining room behind Mary. One long table is filled with nuns, nuns who wear black habits. Another table, twice as long, has the nuns, who like Mary, wear white habits, all novices, I suspect. And then, at two long tables are seated girls, like myself, some younger, some older. At one table, the younger ones sit. At the other, there appear to be girls from perhaps ten years of age to sixteen years of age, all dressed alike. I feel sorely out of place in my blue dress. Mary said I would receive new clothes tomorrow. I feel all their eyes on me as I enter the room. There are a few whispers, but they cease upon hearing one of the nuns, dressed in black, clear her throat.

"Margarita, this is Mary. She is new. She will sit next to you," Mary says, pulling out a chair for me. Margarita smiles. I do my best to smile back as I take my seat.

~~~~

Two years have passed. Today is my fourteenth birthday, although birthdays are not celebrated here. But Margarita, who is also my age, wished me a happy birthday. Margarita, ever since my first day here, has been my best friend. We confide everything to each other. At least Margarita confides everything to me. Although I sometimes talk to her about my mama, I never speak of what happened with my papa.

It took a year before I stopped being jumpy and startled at every sound that differed from my regular routine here. I was always looking over my shoulder, thinking he would find me. My only infraction ever happened about six months into my stay at the convent, when a monk came up behind me, asking where he might find a particular nun. The sound of a male voice caused me to let out a scream. I was busy down on my hands and knees scrubbing the stones on the kitchen floor, lost in thought, dreaming of Mother Mary, and how I so would like to be like her. I received six whacks on each hand with my hair brush, the one they gave me when I arrived.

The punishment came from Mother Isabella. She was the nun most likely to hand out any kind of disciplinary action. I learned to keep my head down, as did most of the girls, whenever she was anywhere near. In my two years here, though, Mother Superior said my conduct has been exemplary. That made me smile. Sometimes Mother Superior reminds me of my mama. I so want to please her.

Margarita's behavior has not been so exemplary. She is more cavalier in her attitude towards the nuns. After all, she has been with them since she was a baby. She has known no other life. She has recently taken a keen interest in the opposite sex and has snuck off more than once to spy on the boy's orphanage. Once she was caught. Mother Isabella considered that a much worse infraction than my own. Margarita showed me the welts on her buttocks. They made me flinch. She slept on her stomach for a whole week. Still, she said it was well worth it.

Margarita doesn't understand why I'm not interested in boys. She calls me well-endowed and confesses she is jealous, although she says she would never confess such a thing in the confessional chamber. My endowment, as she calls it, is something I've always regarded with shame. While Margarita longs to get out in the world and find a husband and have children, I long to hide my body under the robes of a nun. Margarita says I'm crazy.

Because of my exemplary behavior, I have been moved up from kitchen duty. While most of the girls find working in the kitchen deplorable, I don't mind it. I found no task too disgusting. I often hummed while I worked, even while carrying out slop. I think it is for this reason that Mother Superior said I might lead choir for the young children. It was later on that I found my love of song was not the only reason. In fact, she had an ulterior motive.

~~~~

Almost two more years have passed. I have grown to love the young children. I hope to become a novice and a teacher at the convent. I have discussed this with Mother Superior, and she has reminded me in our few conversations that nuns take vows of poverty, obedience, and chastity. I detect a sadness in her eyes during her pronouncement of the word *chastity*. Although I sense nothing but forgiveness in her voice, still I feel dirty. She only says, "Let's wait a while longer. Perhaps you might change your mind." I know I won't, but I certainly don't challenge her on this. I am too meek. Meekness is one of my virtues. Mother Superior has complimented me on this, as well.

There are times when I'm alone that I scrub my body until I feel raw. It has been many years now, but I can't wash the shame away. Margarita doesn't have a clue. She has talked of nothing but the opposite sex for the last couple of years. So, I'm quite surprised when she does a complete turn around and announces to me that she has applied to Mother Superior to become a novice. Now, I am the one who is envious, although I know envy is a sin.

~~~~

It has been two months, and now Margarita wears the robe of a novice. She is in silence. I miss her. Whenever we pass in the corridor I smile, and she extols a brief smile and hurriedly goes on about her business.

My sixteenth birthday is approaching. The thought frightens me. If I'm not allowed to become a nun, I will be turned away. The nuns will try to secure a place for me out in the world, working as a servant, no doubt. More than likely in a Catholic home with children. Mother Superior says I'm good with children.

I see Mother Superior one day in the corridor. She tells me

there is a soldier standing by the North wall. He is a beggar and wants food. I am to go to the kitchen, prepare a plate, and take it to him. The thought of doing this makes me tremble. I also wonder why this order is directly coming from Mother Superior. It is highly unordinary. I think possibly it's a test, a test of obedience. Perhaps I will be selected as a novice after all. I curtsy and say, "Oui, Mother Superior." There is something in her eyes I can't quite make out. It was the same thing I sensed when she gave me charge over the children's choir.

I do my best to steady my nerves, silently saying the prayer I have said so often since I've been here, the one my mother taught me, as I make my way to the kitchen.

Hail, Mary! Full of grace,
The Lord is with thee,
Blessed are thou among women,
and blessed is the fruit of thy womb, Jesus.
Holy Mary, Mother of God,
pray for us sinners,
now, and at the hour of our death.
Amen.

This particular prayer may not be the most appropriate, but this is the one I first learned, the one my mama taught me, and I need to remember her more than ever at the moment. Except for the one incident with the monk, I have managed to avoid any contact with the opposite sex since arriving. There is the exception of the confessional booth, but the priest is behind a curtain, and I imagine his voice of being that of Jesus.

I keep saying the prayer over and over in my head on my walk toward the kitchen. The North wall is near the kitchen. Why didn't someone from the kitchen give the begging soldier food? None of this makes sense. I tell myself it has to be a test.

"I'm here to prepare a plate of food for the beggar." The nun nods as if she has been expecting me. She fixes what had been served earlier for lunch onto a tin plate, adding a couple of biscuits, and tells me to grab a tin cup on my way out. I must have stood there a little too long. "Well, off with you, child."

My teeth are chattering, and I try to hide that fact. We are in the month of August. I try to hold my hands steady as I take the plate from her.

His back is turned away from me as I approach him. My knees feel weak. Why can't he just turn and take the food and let me be off? But, he is looking at some horses that are hitched to a post in the courtyard. He stands near a pile of hay. I clear my throat, "Monsieur, Monsieur." I hold out the plate, using all of my determination not to shake. He turns abruptly, almost causing me to spill the food.

"Oh, oh, I did not mean to startle you," he says.

I look down. His hand, rough and large, touch my fingertips as he takes the plate. "Merci," he says. I bow, and start to walk away.

"The cup," he calls out. I forgot. I still had the tin cup in my hand. I stop in my tracks. I slowly turn and walk back toward him, extending the cup out. "There is water from the pump around the corner," I say, running my words together, almost in a mumble.

"Merci," he says again.

I run back into the kitchen. The nun looks at me in surprise. "Well, don't let him run away with our plate and cup. You must wait until he finishes and retrieve it." I feel myself getting weak but keep saying the prayer over and over in my head, all the while thinking I must pass this test. It is the only way I will ever become a novice. And then I will become a nun. Then, I may occasionally have to deal with a monk or priest, but by then, I will be married to God and will be well equipped to handle it. Just like Mary and Mother Superior.

She shakes her head in annoyance. "Off with you," she says.

I return to the courtyard where he sits on the ground, taking his time chewing each bite with a careful precision. "You're back," he says.

I nod and stand at a respectable distance, hoping he scarfs

down the food at a much faster rate, but he doesn't. Instead, he sees this as an opportunity to talk while he eats. "Nice day," he says.

I nod.

"You don't talk much, do you," he says, sopping up the gravy with his biscuit.

I stand, frozen.

"Hmm," he says, lifting the biscuit to his mouth, as if in contemplation. Although, I'm not looking, I can feel his eyes on me, looking me up and down, perhaps resting his eyes on my bosom. I tense up.

I find myself counting to ten, over and over. I have a habit of counting. That and prayers make tasks easier. With each break before starting over, I glance toward his plate to see how much food he has consumed. Little. I thought he was hungry, but he seems to want to dawdle.

"Do you need to be somewhere?" he asks.

Words don't come. I keep my head down. Fifteen minutes must have passed, fifteen minutes that seem like an hour. He gets up and hands me the empty plate and the tin cup. I take them and run back inside. I hear him call out, "Merci beaucoup."

My heart pounds on the other side of the door as I stop to catch my breath. I feel all eyes are on me as I hand the plate back to the nun and hurry back down the corridor.

~~~~

A week has passed since the incident. I do my best to put it behind me. I am teaching the children a new song. All is well at the moment. I am calmest when I am with the children. Mother Superior enters the room. She sometimes likes to hear the children sing. But, she is observing me. I can tell. After the song, I dismiss the children and she approaches. "The soldier is back," she says. "Might you fix him another plate?"

Of course it is not a question, but a polite command. This is surely a test. I curtsy and try to show no fear, as I say, "Oui, Mother Superior." I feel her eyes perusing me as if she is trying to decide something.

I hurry toward the kitchen, saying once again, the same prayer.

Hail, Mary! Full of grace,
The Lord is with thee,
Blessed are thou among women,
and blessed is the fruit of thy womb, Jesus.
Holy Mary, Mother of God,
pray for us sinners,
now, and at the hour of our death.
Amen.

I feel as if it is the hour of my death. I pray for braveness. I pray I can pass this test. It will merely be a repeat of last week, I tell myself. That was a rehearsal. I will do everything the same, except more calmly. I feel my lunch from earlier trying to come back up my throat, but I swallow it back down.

The same nun hands me the plate full of food. She places a spoon on top. I look down. Is there more this time? He eats so slowly. This will take longer. Once again, she tells me to grab one of the tin cups from the cupboard. I comply.

He is standing in the courtyard in the same place. Except today he is looking at me as I approach. I extend the plate and mug out to him, trying to avoid his touch. "Merci," he says before sitting down amidst the hay. "You remembered the spoon, today." He smiles. I remember how he ate with his hand before. How could I have been so neglectful? Perhaps the spoon will help him eat faster.

I stand silently as he eats.

"Are you not allowed to talk here or something?" he asks. "I've been around maidens in convents before. Most love to talk. But not you. You're different."

I take a heavy breath. This time is different. I wonder why it has to be so. I just want him to leave, but he eats even more slowly with the spoon. I blurt out, "Why are you here? Why are you not off fighting with the other soldiers?"

"Oh," he looks startled. "You can speak." He looks down at his plate and sops up the gravy with his biscuit before looking back up at me. "I am tired of fighting. I just want to settle down and start a family. You are so pretty. Has anyone ever told you that? You have the bluest eyes."

I turn and run. I run through the kitchen and back down the corridor toward the classroom. There is no one there. I slump down in the corner and break down in sobs. It is the first time I've cried since the first day I came here. I didn't even break into tears on the day Mother Isabella whacked my hands with my brush. Will she whack me again for this disobedience? Will I have welts on my buttocks and have to sleep on my stomach? If so, it is worth it. My lunch comes up.

~~~~

Another week passes. Nothing has been said to me. There have been no reprisals. All is back to normal. The children's singing is heavenly. They have mastered the song I taught them last week and will be ready to perform it at mass. I am pleased with myself. I know I will not become a novice. It is not meant to be. I have prayed and spent hours in meditation and have told myself that Mother Mary and my mama in heaven will take care of me.

As the children are leaving, I see Mother Superior standing at the door. "Mary, I wish to talk to you."

I am optimistic. I tell myself my prayers have been answered, and that Mother Superior is the messenger who delivers the answer to the prayer. I stand, humbly, in her presence.

"Oui, Mother Superior." I curtsy.

"The soldier that was here last week," she begins. I suddenly feel faint but use all the power at my disposal to contain myself erect in her presence. She eyes me up and down before continuing, "As I was saying, the soldier that was here last week has expressed an interest in you."

Although, I do my best not to become alarmed, I know my

eyes have widened in question or in fright. "An interest, Mother Superior?"

"Yes, child." She has not called me child in a long while. "He would like to take a wife. I have talked to him at length, and I think he would make a good husband for you."

Although I know it is wrong, I settle down into the chair. I cannot help myself, and I cannot hold back the tears. "Mother Superior, I don't understand. Haven't I done everything that was ever asked of me and even more? I know I would have to either start practicing to become a nun or leave at some point. If I can't become a nun, I thought I might work in a nice home, where there are children," I pleaded, "You know I am good with children. You said so yourself."

"Mary, Mary." She patted me on the head. It was the first time she ever touched me. I saw the pity in her eyes, as she continued to pat my head. She pulled up a chair and sat beside me. "Mary, child." There was the word *child* again. I hadn't heard it in so long. But, I'm not a child, and I have to face that fact.

"Mary, I know you had hopes of living out your life here. And believe me, I have prayed about it. I pray for all of our girls here. As you might have guessed, I have taken a special interest in you. When you first came to us," she stutters for a moment. So unlike Mother Superior. "When you came to us, I suspected what might have happened to you. It was shortly after your father came to me that my suspicions were confirmed. That is when I put you in charge of the children's choir. And it has done wonders for you. I see the way you light up around the children."

"My papa came to you?" This knowledge caused the tears that were flowing down my cheeks to stop mid-track.

"Yes, Mary. I realize your father did unspeakable things to you. He came to us in great remorse. Of course, knowing what we knew, we could not hand you back over to him. He gave the convent a sum of money for your keep. Of course, we take children in all of the time without payment, but the church is not going to turn down donations. Your father was a broken man and had been carrying around a burden of great sorrow. He continued to pay a monthly sum, up until last month."

"Last month?" I say.

"Yes, Mary. Word has come to us that your father passed away while working in the field."

I let out a wail as the tears proceeded to fall again. Why this was happening, I didn't know. All I ever wanted was to get away from him. Suddenly, the stories he used to tell me before my mother passed came back, his smile, his happiness when she was alive. We were happy when Mama was alive.

Mother Superior rises. I feel her hand on my shoulder, as I hold my head down in grief. "There, there, child. It's okay. Let it out. It has been long overdue."

She waits until my tears begin to vanish before continuing. "We understand that your father owned a small farm."

"Oui, Mother," I answer.

"With a husband you can claim that property. The soldier, Mary, who was here, I think he will make you a fine husband. I have always had a good eye for these types of situations. Father Jacob told me this very thing when I was the age you are now. That is the reason I'm over the orphanage. I only want to see all of my girls happy. But, Mary, you are no longer a girl. You are a woman, and, I know you would make a fine mother. And, you need more than anything to get over this fear of men you have."

I look up at her. I'm not sure if I'm looking at her in defeat or thankfulness. I think a little of both.

"The soldier is waiting in the courtyard for you," she says. "I know Margarita is in silence, but you were good friends. I am going to make an exception. She will help you pack. May God be with you, child. And, Mary, here. I have been holding these for you." She hands me my mama's prayer beads. More tears well up, good ones.

~~~~

Five years have passed. A midwife stands at the end of my bed. She holds up a howling baby boy. I am smiling. He looks to be healthy. We name him Jacob after the priest who saw the talents that Mother Superior possessed.

This baby was a long time in coming. Mother Superior was right. Gabriel has been a good husband, a kind and patient man. Perhaps it was the name. He has been like an angel looking out for me. He endured my fear of intimacy for the longest time. But now we are blessed. And with a male child. I think I am continuously being tested, but I no longer quake in fear at each test. That is at least something.

Gabe, I call him Gabe now, enters the room. He is holding a pot of red geraniums. He knows how much I love them. They were the first flowers I saw on the day I was rescued by the nuns.

When I am strong enough we will go to market and carry Jacob. I know when Margarita goes, although she is called Sister Margaret now. She has been put in charge of the kitchen. She will be so happy to see our new addition. And, she is always gladdened to tell me about how the children are doing.

Acknowledgments

The stories all have stories behind them.

The lead story, *The Missing Butler,* came about from entering the NYC Midnight short story contest. It's an international contest in which participants are given the genre, a subject and character, as well as a limited amount of time in which to write the story. I was given the genre of mystery, the subject of bank account and the character of a butler. *The Missing Butler* made Honorable Mention in the first round.

While there are some elements of truth in all of the stories, they are mostly the result of my off beat and sometimes irreverent humor, imagination and never ending questions about life's big and small mysteries.

Two of the stories, *The Wickham* and *Master of the Stacks* (different versions), have been previously published in *Stories from the Stacks* by Wicked Wordsmiths of the West. These stories both have library themes with the character of Burns. The story, *The Plans,* came about from some pretty bizarre writing prompts given at one of the Wicked Wordsmith meetings.

I am especially appreciative of my beta readers, Kim Daniels,

Brenda Ricker, Barbara Chambers and Marsha Blevins. Their evaluations and insights helped greatly. Also, I want to thank my editor, Emerald Barnes.

While I was working on compiling this collection of short stories into a book, my first art teacher, Mr. Larry Carroll, passed away. I was in his first group of art students. Art has always been my first love. I want to thank Larry Carroll for his inspiration and never-ending dedication to his art students and his community.

About the Author

J. Schlenker, a late blooming author, lives with her husband, Chris, out in the splendid center of nowhere in the foothills of Appalachia in Kentucky where the only thing to disturb her writing is croaking frogs and the occasional sounds of hay being cut in the fields. Her first novel, *Jessica Lost Her Wobble*, published in December 2015, was selected as a finalist in the William Faulkner - William Wisdom Creative Writing Competition and won a Five Star Readers Choice Award. One of her short stories, *The Missing Butler*, received honorable mention in the first round of the NYC Competition. *The Color of Cold and Ice* is her second novel.

Upcoming Works are:

The Innkeeper on the Edge of Paris

Sally

Made in the USA
Charleston, SC
12 December 2016